THE VOW

THE DEADLY DECISIONS COLLECTION

D.L. WOOD

SILVERGLASS
PRESS

THE VOW
Copyright ©2022 by D.L. Wood
All rights reserved.

THE VOW is a work of fiction. Names, characters, places, and incidents either are the product of the author's imagination or are used fictitiously. Any resemblance to actual persons, living or dead, events or locales is entirely coincidental and beyond the intent of either the author or publisher.

No part of this book may be reproduced or transmitted in any form or by any means, electronic or mechanical, including photocopying, recording, or by any information storage and retrieval system, without the written permission of the author, except where permitted by law.

ISBN: 9798375230740
First edition
Silverglass Press
Huntsville, Alabama

D.L. Wood
www.dlwoodonline.com

*To Ron on the 28th anniversary of our vows.
Thank you for being the best decision I ever made.*

1

Kate Palmer stopped on the sidewalk, turned around, and listened. For the second time as she walked up her street, she thought she sensed something. Like...someone watching her. A feeling she knew altogether too well.

She shifted the unwieldy package in her arms, her blond hair whipping in the brisk December wind. The light snow that started in the early afternoon was still coming down, sprinkling her with white.

What had she sensed, exactly? Footsteps? Movement? Had she unconsciously registered a glimpse of someone furtively following her? It was more a feeling than anything concrete. But—just like five minutes ago when she had the same feeling—she didn't spot anything amiss. Pedestrians traversed the sidewalks, and cars rolled down the street. But no one seemed to be paying her any particular attention.

Paranoid.

Heat flared at the back of her neck. She didn't like the

jumpy version of herself she had become since one of her clients turned stalker a couple of years ago. Though the restraining order had dealt with it as far as she knew, and she hadn't seen him since, she still had moments of anxiety. Feelings of being watched.

But they aren't true. He isn't here.

Purposely taking the wayward feelings captive, she willed them away and resolutely began walking again.

The flurries that had blanketed the Nashville community of Germantown with a quarter inch of snow muffled the sound of her boot heels on the concrete. She loved the snow and felt a smile cross her face. By the time she reached home, the giddy anticipation of the holiday had taken hold again, all nerves forgotten.

Kate stopped at her front walk, admiring the narrow three-story house she adored. The off-white siding and black-trim structure was even more inviting with the red-ribboned evergreen wreath on the door and colored lights wrapped around the porch.

I love Christmas.

Her heart warmed as she thought of her husband Erik inside, cooking up another masterpiece of a dinner.

Now if I can only get the package in the house without him noticing.

This gift was a last-minute find. An extra special surprise for Christmas morning. She had bought and wrapped Erik's and everyone else's presents weeks ago. But when her schedule unexpectedly cleared that afternoon, she couldn't resist indulging in some last-minute, festive holiday shopping before Erik got home. So she had buttoned-up her wool coat and walked from their house to the eclectic shops and eateries at the heart of Germantown, just blocks away.

With a cup of cinnamon-laced hot chocolate from the cafe on the corner in hand, she eventually landed in the art gallery she and Erik often visited on their Saturday strolls. Its quirky, original pieces always captured Erik's attention and that afternoon she struck gold, snagging a bold oil canvas by a local artist he admired. The contemporary piece, with its primary colors contrasted against smooth, circular strokes, was a vivid work she knew Erik would love to have hanging in his psychiatry office.

In their five years of marriage, he had always been the one to surprise *her* with some unexpected, thoughtful present on Christmas.

This year, it's my turn.

Chuckling, Kate marched up her brick front steps. She set the large framed canvas down gently, retrieved her keys and quietly unlocked the door.

I'll hide it in the hall closet for now. Then later, when he's asleep, I'll sneak it upstairs into the closet of the spare bedroom.

She wasn't too worried about him catching her coming in. Erik would be distracted in the kitchen, his favorite jazz station—*no, at this time of year it'll be Christmas classics*—blaring. Early in their marriage, he had assumed the role of preparing meals as she was hopeless in the kitchen, unless you were talking about decorating it, or any other room in any house. *That* she excelled in, and was the reason interior decorating became her career. But after burning more meals than not, they decided he would cook and she would clean up, which suited her just fine.

She imagined him now, his wavy auburn hair brushed so that the ends still stuck out here and there. His close-trimmed mustache and beard. And him singing along with the music horribly—the man couldn't carry a tune to save his life—while he worked away in that awful, spattered apron he refused to wash.

But as she noiselessly shut and locked the door behind her, the first thing she noticed was the absolute quiet. No music. No utensils clanking. Nothing. The next thing that struck her was the absence of aroma. Erik's cooking typically made their home smell like a five-star restaurant, or a grandmother's kitchen, depending on the fare. Tonight, though, only the faint scent of evergreen drifted into the foyer, originating from the decorated Fraser fir in the family room.

Concern needled her. If Erik wasn't in the kitchen, he could be anywhere. She moved quickly, tucking the package in the closet. She removed her coat, hung it inside and closed the door with a gentle click.

"Erik?" she called, removing her boots. "You here?"

Nothing.

Was he upstairs?

"Erik?"

Still no answer.

If he was upstairs, he should have heard her. The house might be three stories tall, but it was only 2100 square feet. The draw for them had not been the size of the home, but its location. Two years ago they fell in love with it on their first walk-through and made an offer on the spot, despite the strain on their budget.

Not that they didn't do all right for themselves. His psychiatry practice now had a waiting list, and the clientele of her boutique decorating firm included some of country music's elite. But as they were both only thirty and still had his medical school loans to pay, there was little discretionary income. The house was an extravagant purchase, but neither ever voiced doubts about it. They had the life they wanted in a city they loved with their favorite haunts just a five-minute walk away.

Besides, they had years to save.

Kate crossed the black-and-white tiled foyer, then headed down the hallway leading into the combined kitchen and living area at the back of the house.

"Erik?" She could hear the slight urgency in her voice now, born more out of curiosity than anything. Was he up to something? His own Christmas surprise, maybe?

A walkway divided the kitchen and family room, with a leather L-shaped couch to the right and a large island that served as table and preparation counter on the left. The gas stove gleamed, devoid of pots and pans. No dinner and no Erik.

But the white lights on their tree were twinkling, the gold and silver ornaments Kate had carefully chosen sparkling, casting a cozy glow around the space. So he *was* there. Or at least had been there long enough to turn on the tree.

She bounded upstairs for a quick check of those floors, thinking maybe he was napping, but he wasn't there either. Kate slid her hand along the wrought iron banister as she made her way back down the wooden stairs, checking her phone.

But there wasn't a single text from him.

Maybe he got an emergency call and had to go back to the

office? Did he come home and have the same idea about last-minute shopping?

Her lips pursed. Seems like he would've texted her, though, after seeing *her* car at home. She opened the *Find My iPhone* app, her finger moving to the bottom of her phone's screen, ready to press his name to see his location. Only his name wasn't there. Somehow he had been removed from her "People" contacts. Her face scrunched in confusion.

What is going on?

She tapped on her phone again.

> Hey. Where r u? I'm home. Want me to order takeout?

She hit send, then waited for a response. But none came.

Kate's gut prickled, a burgeoning worry taking hold until suddenly she sighed, feeling like an idiot.

The shed. Of course.

A small detached storage shed sat adjacent to their rear driveway. Sometimes Erik worked on projects in there... although it was a little cold for that.

Unless it's one of his surprises.

Kate stepped outside through the family room's back door, the chilly air biting her skin, her feet quickly feeling the sting of the cold, as she hadn't thought to put her boots back on. She hustled to the shed and knocked, calling out his name as she jiggled the door handle.

Locked.

Putting aside any concern over spoiling surprises, she stood on her tiptoes to peer through the decorative glass in the top of the door. He wasn't inside. Effecting an awkward hop-walk to limit her feet contacting the snow, she went back in the house and ripped off her damp socks.

A fire.

I'll light a fire, order takeout and just wait.

She pulled up the menu from one of their favorite Chinese places.

It actually makes sense that he's not texting.

If he's with a patient, he can't talk. Or, if he's gone on his own surprise shopping excursion, he obviously wouldn't want me to know where he—

And that's when she saw it—a white envelope, tucked in the branches of their Christmas tree, her name on it in Erik's familiar scrawl. She plucked it out, the tree's needles scratching the back of her hand.

She felt her grin return. He *was* planning something.

A flight somewhere for the Christmas holiday?

A cruise?

Or...no...it couldn't be.

Bubbly anticipation percolated in her stomach.

Was he planning a holiday jaunt to their Smoky Mountains cabin? They both loved the quiet, rustic nature of the place she had inherited from her grandfather. Even now, just thinking of its hewn wooden beams and roaring fireplace conjured deep, heartfelt family memories in Kate. She and Erik had grand plans for updating it, and they often talked about going there for Christmas.

Is this finally the year?

Kate slid a manicured finger beneath the envelope's flap,

extracted a single sheet of Erik's professional letterhead, and began to read. Ice seized her center, then mercilessly exploded into the farthest reaches of her soul.

Kate,
I can't live like this anymore...

2

ONE YEAR LATER

You never really know someone.

These words echoed in Kate Palmer's mind, as they had thousands of times over the last year. Her Acura SUV flew east down the straight stretch of I-40 from Nashville to East Tennessee, gray, moisture-laden skies hovering above as her best friend's voice filled the interior over Bluetooth.

"I still don't see why you have to go there for Christmas," Holly Ishida remarked, undisguised frustration in her voice. The comment pulled Kate from her reverie, and she pictured her business partner, wrinkles of distaste likely crossing her face as she ran graceful hands through her shiny black hair.

"I'm not calling for a lecture, Holly. I just wanted to check on the plans for the Merrick House."

"Met with them an hour ago. They were thrilled. We've got the job," she reported with monotone precision. "So tell me again why you have to go to the middle-of-nowhere all by yourself two days before Christmas?"

"I have to prep the cabin for sale."

"You don't have to do it over Christmas."

"My real estate agent says differently."

Holly harrumphed. "I don't believe you."

Kate heaved a sigh. "He said the cabin needs to be on the market by January first if I want any chance of selling it in time to pay the settlement by the deadline—"

"Then go any time after this week. Come on, Kate. This is crazy. You don't want to spend Christmas alone. That's depressing. Your family wants you with them—"

The image of Kate's childhood home in Asheville, North Carolina, flashed through her mind, along with a vision of her family festively gathered in front of the tree: Mom and Dad, her sister and brother with their happy spouses and their respective little ones running around. Her insides clenched. "I just can't."

"Instead, you're spending it in the place you and your ex-husband wanted to spend Christmas? How is that less depressing?"

"It was *my* place before it was going to be *our* place. My grandfather left it to me. I wanted to spend Christmas there after I inherited the place from Pop, and I never did. If I don't do it now, I never will."

Silence filled the SUV's cabin as snowflakes began hitting the windshield more ferociously. After two-and-a-half hours of driving, with the elevation increasing, the powder was really coming down. She flipped her wipers to a higher speed.

Holly sighed. "I just can't stand the thought of you up there, in the mountains, freezing and alone, crying your eyes out over that complete jerk."

"It's not about him. And I need to do this. I need to say goodbye to the place."

The Vow

"I still don't get why you have to sell it. You must have other options to raise the money to pay him off."

"I really don't." But, oh, how she wished she did. More than anything she wanted to hang onto the cabin where her grandparents had lived. The place where she had spent so many summers. It just wasn't possible. "Look, it boils down to the reality that I can't afford the Germantown place by myself. I could sell it, and give Erik his half, but that's never going to happen. I'm not giving him the satisfaction. He may have ripped my world to shreds, but he's not kicking me out of my own home. Unless I sell the cabin, I don't have enough cash to buy Erik out *and* get the mortgage down to something manageable on my salary alone. You know this."

Kate hated talking about the financial issues she was facing because of the divorce. It was her business, and she didn't want anyone offering handouts or pitying her. Not Holly and especially not her family. She and Erik hadn't known each other long before they married, and her family hadn't been very supportive of the decision. Now, after what he had done, getting help from them would have been more than embarrassing.

No. This was her mess. She had made this bed. Now she had to lie in it.

"So, in reality, he *is* kicking you out of your home," Holly said acidly. "Or your cabin at least."

"Well, I can't keep both. And I rarely get up there so it makes sense to let it go. I guess I just can't have it all anymore."

"But he gets to?" Holly fired back, her words laced with disgust.

She wasn't wrong. Erik had walked away from their life,

leaving her to handle the dismantling of it. Papers served and letters sent by his lawyer dictated the terms—or at least Erik's terms—of the divorce. Not only had he left as cruelly as possible, blindsiding her completely, but by keeping her in the dark he was able to clean half the money out of their accounts before she knew what hit her. They were cash poor anyway, which meant she had to sell something to stay afloat. There was no way she was letting go of the Germantown house. So the cabin it was.

Meanwhile, he was off, traveling the globe, flitting around with his new trust-fund wife.

New wife.

The thought of it sucked the air out of her lungs, and she gripped the steering wheel for strength.

"Kate?" Holly asked, her voice tentative. "You there?"

"Yeah. Just thinking about him having it all." Thanks to social media, she had a front row seat to Erik's new life, new wife and "kept" existence. Miranda Townsend—Miranda Palmer as of three months ago—was a former patient and apparently a trust fund twenty-five-year-old with more money than she and Erik could spend, despite how hard they were trying. Their regular Instagram posts were gut-wrenching... Barbados, the Florida Keys, Turks and Caicos—

"Kate, whatever thought spiral you're in, stop."

Holly was right. She wasn't going to let him do this to her. She shook her head, resetting her thoughts. "You're right. I'm okay."

"He isn't worth it."

"No, he's not," Kate agreed.

"Not one more minute of your life wasted on him. Right?"

"Right." Kate had made that vow to Holly one night as she

cried on her friend's shoulder, packing up the last of Erik's things to be shipped to his new place in Charleston. That was six months ago. She hadn't always been able to keep that promise. But she was trying.

The exit for I-140, the highway that would usher her to the Great Smoky Mountains, appeared on the right. She veered into the turn lane, then stepped on the gas out of the curve. Only another forty minutes and she would be on the back roads leading to the cabin.

"So there's no talking you out of it?" Holly asked.

"I wish there was...but, no."

"Well, I hope you find whatever you're looking for there," her friend said gently.

"I'm looking for goodbye," Kate said, the lonely truth stabbing her in the heart afresh. "There isn't anything else anymore."

3

She turned off the interstate, and he turned, following her. He was confident she hadn't noticed him. He stayed several cars back, and the snow and fairly heavy traffic had provided plenty of cover up to this point. That would change, though, the closer she got to her destination. The roads would narrow. The traffic would lessen. Then he would have to pull even farther back. But for now he was safe.

She couldn't say the same.

4

After turning off the interstate, the foothills of the Smokies opened up before Kate along the darkening horizon. But with each turn onto another rural highway, she sank deeper into the backwoods of eastern Tennessee, slowly closing out the distant vista. Now the trees and undergrowth pressed in close against the road, creating living walls that hemmed her in on both sides, offering only a view of what lay directly ahead.

The cabin sat in Bloodroot Ridge, a secluded community named for the spring-blooming white flower indigenous to the area. It was roughly forty miles south of Knoxville, not far from the southwest entrance of the Foothills Parkway that ran along the edge of the national park. There was a distinct lack of commercial presence here; she had passed the last gas station five miles back. Now there were only cabins and other single-family dwellings with none of the planned communities common in Gatlinburg and other touristy areas. Privacy was valued and protected here. It was part of what her grandparents had loved about the place and something that had drawn Kate to it as well. That, and the peace that existed there —just the cabin and nature. A quiet refuge from...well, whatever storm was raging. It was a balm. And she needed it.

Even if it was only this one last time.

She sucked in a deep breath, struck by a sudden urgency to finally be there. And almost in that same moment, she saw it—the green mailbox at the end of the cabin's long dirt drive.

She turned in, speeding up the drive faster than was prudent in the heavy snow, but not caring. She braked hard as she reached the end, put the SUV in park, and leaned both arms on the wheel, taking in the structure illuminated by her headlights.

The red cedar plank cabin consisted of two stories. The front door was squarely in the center of the bottom story with a small porch and large window to its left. The upper story was one loft that stretched down the cabin's entire length, its ceiling forming the upside-down "V" roofline. Above the porch was the narrow balcony of the second floor, with a wooden-slat railing and a sliding glass door leading inside. She was glad to see the porch light shining, likely left on for her by the cleaning service she had hired to prepare the place for her stay.

A rush of emotion broke over Kate as she stared at the old cabin, the place where so many memories of her past and hopes for her future had resided. Suddenly she was out of her car, jogging to the front door, no coat, no bags, her boots pounding on the wooden steps. She jammed her key in the lock, opened the door and stepped inside.

Leaving the frigid wind and snow at her back, she shut

the door, then turned on the small lamp sitting on the entryway table. Dim lamplight combined with light filtering through the window from the porch fixture spilled over the room. It looked exactly as she remembered. Nothing had changed.

Kate's throat felt raw, and she choked back tears. She could almost pretend that, here, time had stopped in some blissful moment *before* that terrible day one year ago. Unbidden memories of her youth bubbled up one after the other, as if trying to reclaim this place as part of her, not a tainted reminder of the failure that had been her marriage. Of how stupid and naive she had been. Of how foolish and blind she was to trust Erik.

Erik.

Kate's battling emotions swelled, a heady dizziness setting in until her legs refused to support her. She crumpled to the floor, a heap of sorrow and wasted dreams, curled on the rug her grandmother had placed there decades before, and sobbed.

Kate woke with a start, jerking as her eyes flew open, her heart banging wildly in her chest. Disoriented, she pushed herself into a sitting position on the floor. She took a deep breath and surveyed the room.

You're in the cabin.

How long have I been out?

Kate reached in her pocket for her phone, then remembered she left it in the car.

I must have been really out of it. Otherwise, how would she have been able to sleep on that hard floor? Plus, she felt heavy and groggy, familiar after-effects of waking from a dead sleep.

If I was that far gone, what woke me?

She stood, intending to hit the switch on the wall for the overhead light, when her gaze passed across the sheers covering one of the windows on the side of the cabin.

A face, draped in shadows, peered in at her.

Kate's scream pierced the air.

At her wail, the face disappeared into the void. Kate's heart drummed wildly in her ears, her breath coming in quick gasps as she raced toward the window, then stopped herself mere feet away.

She needed to get a look at whoever was out there, but was it safe to get close to the window? What if they were still just on the other side, waiting?

Her need to know outweighed her fear, and she charged forward, yanking back the sheers.

No one.

Not at the window and not as far as she could see into the grounds. But there were footprints in the snow leading away from the window, eventually blurring into the darkness.

Had the person truly run off? Or were they just waiting out of sight?

With her phone in the car, Kate couldn't call for help. But that didn't mean she was helpless. Stepping quickly behind the couch, she moved to the trunk shoved against its back, selected a small key from her keyring, and unlocked it. Reaching inside, she extracted her grandfather's rifle and a box of bullets, then loaded the weapon.

She squinted at the microwave in the kitchen across the way.

2:37 a.m.

Still shaking with nervous energy, she drew the curtains closed, then sank into the couch so that she was facing both the front door and the window where the face had appeared. Gripping the rifle in one hand, she wrapped a fuzzy throw around herself with the other and willed daylight to come.

5

Knock-knock. Knock-knock-knock-knock.

The repetitive banging was relentless, this time leaving Kate no doubt about what had woken her. She blinked, adjusting to the daylight streaming through the sheers, all the more brilliant because of the snow blanketing the ground. Hopping up off the couch, she brandished the rifle and moved to the window beside the front door. Angling herself to avoid being seen, she pulled the curtains back just a fraction, then grinned.

After propping the gun against the wall, she swung the door wide. "Georgia!" Kate exclaimed, and held her arms out to the early thirty-something woman dressed in jeans and a gray pullover, with straight sleek hair the color of mink and sparkling green eyes.

"Kate!" the woman replied with equal glee and dove in for an enthusiastic hug. When she finally stepped back, Kate was still grinning. It had been more than a year and a half since she had seen her childhood friend.

The Vow

"I didn't know you were coming!" Georgia exclaimed. "When I saw the cleaners here last week, I thought you were prepping the house for sale."

"I am. I was. But...I wanted to come out one last time, you know? Say goodbye. Pack up some of the personal things before the movers come in to do the rest." A gust of cold wind reminded Kate they were standing in the doorway. "Sorry! Come in," Kate apologized, ushering Georgia inside and to the couch.

The Cranes had bought the property next door and built a vacation cabin on it when Kate was in elementary school, though the term "next door" was a sizable understatement. Their respective properties were roughly four acres-plus each, so in truth, nothing was really next-door to either of them. But they were each other's closest neighbor, fifty yards of thick woods between the cabins.

The girls had played together since the age of eight, thick as thieves every time Kate had visited her grandparents at their cabin. It had made things so much more interesting for Kate to have a friend her own age there. Particularly since her brother and sister were several years older than she was, and in those days didn't want much to do with her. The girls had made the woods their own—exploring, getting lost, camping, fishing—Georgia and her younger brother, Rex, were two of the reasons giving up the cabin would be so hard.

"You should have told me you were coming," Georgia chided. "This is such a great surprise for Christmas."

Kate bit her lip sheepishly. "I should have. But it was a last-minute decision. And I didn't want to interrupt your and Rex's plans for the holidays."

"Oh!" Georgia squealed, "That reminds me. Rex said he

came over here last night. He said he looked in the window and saw you and apparently you screamed or something?"

Kate's hand flew to her chest. "Well, that explains it. I didn't get a good look. Yeah, I was pretty freaked out by it."

Georgia's face scrunched. "Ugh. I'm sorry. Apparently, he was on one of his late-night rambling strolls and saw a light on in the cabin. He knew no one was supposed to be here and wanted to check it out. He didn't tell me about it until this morning."

"I wish he had just knocked when he saw it was me," Kate said.

"He thought you'd be angry he was looking in the windows. He was pretty spooked by it all."

"Poor guy." Kate could easily believe that the episode frightened Rex far more than it had her. Georgia's younger brother was the sweetest, kindest man you could ever meet. But he was also quite shy and skittish, stemming from a mild intellectual difference, which was the reason why, at twenty-seven, he still lived with his sister. Their parents had died in a car accident right after Georgia graduated from high school. After that, she and Rex tried staying in Memphis, where they had lived with their parents—Georgia was a painter and loved that vibe—but the noise and chaos simply overwhelmed Rex too much after the loss. Seeking peace and quiet, they had made the family vacation cabin their home, and Rex had thrived there.

Georgia nodded at the rifle propped against the wall. "Looks like he scared you pretty good."

"I left my phone in the car and couldn't go out, so holing up with that," Kate said, pointing to the gun, "was my only option. Will you tell Rex I'm not mad? Or better yet, send him over later. I'll make some chocolate-chip cookies. I know they're his favorite."

"He'll love that. But I'll give you a chance to settle in and maybe send him over this afternoon?"

Kate nodded. "Perfect. I had the cleaners stock the place for me so—oh, speaking of which," she interrupted herself, jumping off the couch, "coffee?"

"I never turn coffee down," Georgia replied.

Kate got to work in the kitchen, filling the coffeemaker. "You still take it black, no sugar?"

"Bitter and dark, just like my personality."

Kate snorted. That description couldn't be further from Georgia's actual jovial, warm demeanor. Kate had once asked what Georgia was going to do if, when she finally met the man of her dreams, he wasn't up for backwoods living with her younger brother. *"He'll either learn to like it,"* Georgia had said, *"or I guess he won't be that man."*

They drank their coffee and caught up, including a spectacular ten minutes of Georgia skewering Erik and jokingly describing all the ways Kate could take revenge—from hiring a hit-man to dumping the new car he was flaunting on social media in a lake. Kate even pitched a couple of ideas and found herself laughing, something she never did when it came to Erik. She also didn't normally let her friends go on about her ex—too depressing—but talking about it with Georgia was oddly therapeutic.

When their mugs were drained, Georgia said she should probably get back. "You know," she added, pulling back from Kate's goodbye hug in the doorway, "you should come over for Christmas dinner tomorrow."

Kate's heart nose-dived at the thought of having to be

around people on what she expected was going to be a very difficult day. The last thing she wanted was to have to put on a brave face. "I don't know, Georgia," she said and heaved a sigh, leaning on the doorframe. "I'd love to say yes—"

"Then do."

"It's just...Christmas is hard since Erik left. I doubt I'll be good company." She pasted on an apologetic smile. "But why don't you two come over the day after? We could play some games. They should get used one last time before I sell the place."

Georgia smiled sadly. "If you're sure. But the offer stands."

Kate walked her out to the drive, then headed to her SUV for her things. After waving goodbye as Georgia drove off, she gathered her bags and went back in, dropping her suitcase and duffel on the living room floor.

Alone again. She exhaled dejectedly, then froze.

Something was very wrong.

6

A lot of somethings were wrong, actually. She hadn't noticed before. Last night was too dark and this morning she had been distracted by Georgia. Plus they had sat on the couch, facing the front door, their backs to the rest of the cabin. But now, getting a good look at the space in the daylight, it was clear things were just...off.

Three frames holding drawings by elementary age versions of her and her siblings had been switched around. Books between the bookends had been rearranged, "Z" to "A" rather than "A" to "Z," something her grandfather had always insisted upon. A vase moved. The games on the wrong shelf of the bookcase.

Could the cleaners have done this? Moving things to dust made sense, and she had paid them to be extra-thorough as she was putting the place up for sale. But the book rearrangements?

An uneasy prickle crept up Kate's spine, prompting her to lock the front door. She grabbed her bags and headed down the hallway that stretched the entire length of the structure, ending at the master bedroom. On the way, she passed the two spare bedrooms and their shared bath. She paused momentarily before the grouping of graduation photos of every member of the family on one wall. Her stomach lurched. They too had been rearranged.

The cleaners definitely would not have done that. Urgency and unease prodding her on, she strode into the master bedroom that had once been her grandparents' retreat. She had fond memories of playing with her dolls on the rug, jumping with her brother and sister on the bed...Now the room was hers and Erik's—

No. Just mine. Frustration blossomed in the wake of yet another mental slip, even now. *A whole year later.*

Kate's eyes roved around the space as she gently set her bags atop the thick, off-white duvet covering the white-washed pine-frame bed. The room was large and airy, with a sitting area off to the right with cozy armchairs covered in faux fur throws and bay windows that offered an expansive view of the woods frosted with snow.

She surveyed the room for signs of disturbance. Most of her grandparents' personal belongings had been taken from the room when Pop died. But their antique gold mirror still hung over the dresser. And the black-and-white photograph of their wedding day in 1954 hung in its rightful place on the wall over the fireplace.

So maybe I'm wrong. Maybe it was just the cleaners after all, a little overzealous in their efforts.

But then she saw it. Or rather—didn't.

The special spot on her grandmother's vanity where Mama K's crystal perfume bottle and Pop's eyeglasses had resided since Kate had inherited the cabin was empty. Her hands shook as searing anger and a nauseating sense of violation flooded her. Someone had broken into her cabin, touched, rearranged, and *taken* things from her. Precious things.

Why? Why her?

They had walked into this cabin, right into her world, and taken from her.

Someone had stolen what was hers right out from under her.

Again.

The sheriff's deputies arrived within the hour, no lights flashing, sending the message that this was not something they were overly concerned about. After checking the place over, clearing it, and taking Kate's statement, they explained that this sort of thing happened all the time. That cabins left uninhabited for too long often fell victim to burglary. It wasn't unusual.

No, Kate thought bitterly. *Being stolen from wasn't unusual for her.* Having what was hers ripped from her grip without warning was something she was well-acquainted with. At least this time it had just been things. Not a person. Not *her* person.

Then again, these aren't just things.

These were priceless, irreplaceable, personal things. Things worth nothing and everything. At least to her.

The deputies speculated it had been teenagers, pulling teenage stunts. Or a burglar who didn't find anything of value and took what he could, maybe out of frustration. Though Kate wanted to believe either of those scenarios, she wasn't buying it. Because there *had* been valuable things in the cabin that the burglar hadn't bothered with.

For one, there was the trunk. Wouldn't any burglar worth his salt try to break it open at least? See whether anything of value was stored inside? But she found it locked when she retrieved the rifle.

For another, no drawers had been left open, no closets left in disarray after a good ransacking. She had already checked with the cleaners, who found nothing like that. So, if there *was* a burglar, it was the tidiest burglar in history. When she pointed these things out to the deputies, they reverted to the "pranky teenagers" theory. Without much imagination for anything else, they had her sign off on the report, then disappeared in their patrol vehicle.

But Kate wasn't satisfied because, whatever they said, this felt personal. Another personal attack in the most personal of places. And there were only two people in the world who would both understand that *and* go to these lengths to make her feel this violated.

One made bile rise in her throat, her stomach turning in disgust.

The other sent a shiver of fear cascading through her body.

7

That afternoon, Kate stood in her front doorway, embracing Rex in an enthusiastic hug. She pulled back, appraising the six-foot tall, broad, bearded man, suited up in full winter gear. "Did you hike over?"

He nodded.

Of course he had. Given the choice between riding in a car or being in the outdoors, Rex would choose the outdoors every time. "Well, come in," Kate said, pulling on his sleeve, "before you freeze to death."

Minutes later, Rex sat on the couch, staring at a hot cup of tea cradled in his hands. The cup was bone china, part of a Johnson Brothers set Mama K had brought back from a twentieth anniversary trip to England.

Thank you, Lord, they didn't take these. That would've been a tough blow.

Rex said little except for a quiet "thank you" and "these are good" when he accepted a warm chocolate-chip cookie from a china plate adorned with the same pink roses that encircled the rim of his teacup. It looked so tiny in his large hands, calloused from years of working for a local log cabin construction outfit. Normally he was fairly chipper around Kate, so his drawn posture and near silence suggested he was feeling really guilty about the night before. Apparently he hadn't taken the message she sent through Georgia to heart. He hadn't even looked at her properly. Instead he just gave her side glances from beneath a curtain of his dark shoulder-length hair.

Kate's heart melted like the chips in the cookies. *Bless him.* She reached for his hand.

"Rex, if you're worried about last night, you don't need to be. You didn't do anything wrong."

"But you screamed," he said, his words quick and full of regret.

"Only because you—" she switched her approach quickly when his eyes widened at the word *'you'* "—because *I* was startled. If you think about it, you were actually doing me a huge favor."

For the first time, he turned to look at her directly, his green eyes doubtful. "I did?"

Kate nodded. "You were protecting my cabin. You thought someone had broken in and you were brave to check it out."

The crease in his forehead said that he didn't fully believe her, but at least he seemed to be considering it.

"And," Kate continued, "if someone *had* been here, you would have probably scared them off. Which makes you a hero. And makes me feel safer knowing you're right down the road."

The hint of a smile peeked out from the corner of his mouth.

There we go.

"I make you feel safe?"

"You always have. Remember that summer when the tourist boy in the cabin up the road came down here on his bike? He started throwing rocks at me, and I had to run."

It was Rex's turn to nod, a shadow flitting across his face at the memory.

"You knocked him off that bike and told him if he ever came back, he'd be the one running."

A tiny snort escaped Rex, and he raised his teacup, draining it. "He didn't come back."

"No. He didn't." She smiled. "All thanks to you." She let him take that in before continuing. "Georgia said you came over last night because you saw a light on in the cabin."

"Yeah." He tilted his head toward the small lamp on the entryway table. "That one. It's not usually on."

"No. It's not." She swallowed, hoping this wouldn't go over the wrong way. "Rex, have you seen anyone else in the cabin lately, or any other lights or cars that aren't supposed to be here?"

His face flushed pink.

Shoot, he thinks he's in trouble again.

"It's okay if you did. More than okay. I'm actually hoping you did see someone because...well, somebody broke in here, Rex. I don't know when. It could've been a while ago or recently."

He said nothing, but set the cup on the coffee table and held his hands in a tight knot against his legs.

He still thinks he might be in trouble. "I promise you'll be helping if you can tell me anything about seeing anyone here. They moved things around, Rex. And took things. Special things."

"Things that belonged to Pop and Mama K?" Rex lifted his gaze to hers, a darker glint in his eyes. Rex had been close to both her grandparents, continuing that relationship with Pop even after Mama K died. They fished together, hunted, and even woodworked in Pop's shed. Rex wouldn't like someone disturbing their things, and it showed in the hard line his lips had formed.

"Yes. Pop and Mama K."

Rex's eyes glistened a bit. "I'm sorry. I'm sorry that happened."

"Me too. They took his glasses and her perfume bottle. You remember her bottle? I pretended to spray it on Georgia once?"

He nodded. She was sure he did remember. It was an heirloom that once belonged to Mama K's grandmother. Mama K had gotten onto her for playing with it, and Rex had run right out of the cabin, terrified he was in trouble too.

"That's not right," he muttered.

"No, it's not. Life often isn't," Kate replied, throwing an arm around him and side-hugging him. "But I'll be okay. If you think of anything, though, or see anyone else around the cabin that isn't supposed to be here, will you let me know?"

He nodded. "Yeah."

"And don't forget, I owe you one for checking on the cabin last night, okay?"

He glanced up at her from beneath his hanging locks. "One more cookie?"

Kate smiled and squinted. "How about a whole dozen and you keep watching out for me, okay?"

Rex responded with a sharp, two-fingered salute, just the way Pop used to do.

8

It was nearly three o'clock by the time Rex left. Three in the afternoon on Christmas Eve, and Kate hadn't done a thing to make the cabin look like Christmas was coming in less than twelve hours.

"You wanted to spend a Christmas here," she grumbled at herself, heading up the stairs leading to the second-story loft. "Better get at it."

How many times had she gripped the smooth, sanded railing leading to the loft? She and her siblings had played up there, made forts and countless messes, while the adults did whatever adults did downstairs—cooking, watching television, playing card games, talking about a whole lot of nothing. At the top landing, she set her feet on the carpet and surveyed the room that stretched from the front of the cabin to the back, interrupted only by a large closet, a bathroom and the attic storage space at the rear. This room had been their kingdom. And she had hoped one day to transfer ownership of that kingdom to her children.

Yet another dream to let go.

She heaved the millionth sigh since arriving and headed for the attic storage space. A single door in the center of the loft's back wall opened straight into it. It probably could have been used as a bedroom if Pop had finished it, since the space was temperature regulated. But the studs still showed, and the floor was covered with plywood. Storage boxes and plastic tubs stacked at varying heights filled it, and somewhere behind those was a half-circle-shaped window, pouring light in, making the overhead light unnecessary.

Kate's brow furrowed at the number of storage boxes. It was more than she remembered. She had known part of her visit would be spent going through them, deciding what to keep and what to dump. But it looked like it would be a bigger job than expected.

What she did expect was that most of it would get tossed. Anything of significant value—monetary or sentimental—had been divided up by the family after Pop died. Her family had spent a weekend sifting through everything, including all the precious memorabilia and heirlooms. What remained was household paraphernalia no one had wanted, or items Kate and Erik thought they might use in the cabin someday.

Another plan abandoned.

Flipping open the top of the nearest box revealed an extra set of dishes, Tupperware and miscellaneous utensils. Another box held extra blankets. A highchair sat off to one side and next to that, a folding table and chairs. A rolled-up rug...She would go through it all before she left, but she couldn't imagine keeping any of it.

Except for the one thing that had brought her in there.

The tree.

Kate's fond memories of childhood Christmases in the cabin was one of the reasons she had been so keen for Erik and her to enjoy their own Christmases there. Pop and Mama K, Daddy and Mom, Brianna and Shaun. All snuggled up on the couches and chairs, with fuzzy blankets and pajamas before a blazing fire and the tree, its twinkling colored lights sparkling, sending rainbows bouncing off ornaments, filling the room with a vibrant glow.

It was that tree she was going to put up today. That tree that would crown one last Christmas in the Kincaid family cabin. And she would take it with her too, so someday, when this nightmare was well past her and she had started over, she could bring it out again when she had someone to share it with.

So where was it?

It was an eight-foot-high tree, so, even if it had been covered or dismantled for easy moving, it should be easy to spot. Probably sitting right beside whatever storage tub or box held the lights and ornaments. But it wasn't there. Or at least she didn't see it from where she was standing. Things had been moved around a lot when her family came to sift through Pop's stuff.

Must have been laid on the floor behind the stacks.

She moved a mound of three tubs, shifting the heavy containers one by one, stepped through the entryway she created, and gasped.

Laid out in front of the window were several blankets mounded together in a makeshift bed. Beside that was a smaller cardboard box that seemed to be serving as a bedside table. A flashlight sat on top. There was even a plastic grocery bag next to it that held what looked like trash.

The wall of storage boxes hadn't been an accident. Someone had configured them to create and hide this little space. Someone had been *living there.*

As if she needed any more proof, pushed into the corner, previously hidden from view by a particularly high stack of boxes, was the tree. It stood upright, strands of lights wound around it. The precious ornaments from Kate's childhood adorned its needles, including the gold-foil star she had gingerly helped place in Christmases past perched proudly on top.

9

Ice crystallized Kate's insides as she stared at the remnants of what was clearly someone's makeshift campground. Multiple questions, including *who* and *why*, raced through her mind, but the one that made her breath catch was, *were they still here?*

She took several slow breaths to calm her racing heart.

The deputies and I went through the entire house checking for missing items. We didn't find anyone.

Well, not the *entire* house, she challenged. *Because none of us saw this.*

They *had* checked the attic. But it hadn't even occurred to her—and obviously not the deputies either—to look behind the boxes. For one, it was such a small space with the boxes shoved so close to the window, and two, because they weren't really checking for a lingering intruder. They were checking for stolen items.

If they'd missed this, what else—*who else*—had they missed?

A sudden urgency gripping her, Kate opened every box and plastic tub and paced every inch of the attic, but found nothing unexpected. She examined the blankets as closely as she could without touching them. Using a stray hanger, she lifted the grocery bag and found candy wrappers and crushed soda cans inside. She dropped it back on the floor, then took photos of everything.

How long had it been since whoever created the space last stayed there?

Hopefully, a long, long time.

Pop had died four years ago, and her family went through the attic six months after that. The makeshift campsite definitely wasn't there at that time, and though she didn't remember the tree being set up like that, it could have been. It was possible it had never been taken apart after Pop's last Christmas there. That meant as many as three-and-a-half years could have passed since the last intrusion. But something told Kate this was a recent thing. And that it was likely connected with the missing heirlooms.

Whoever was responsible was gone.

What troubled her was whether they planned to come back.

After thoroughly checking the entire house again with the rifle in hand, Kate made a call to the sheriff's department and was connected with the same lead deputy—Deputy Lyle—from that morning. Unsurprisingly, he wasn't particularly hopeful about their chances of discovering who had engineered their own private room in Kate's attic.

"Honestly," Deputy Lyle said, his deep voice sounding resigned, "this only further suggests the items stolen from your place were taken by someone passin' through, using the uninhabited cabin while they could. Now that you're here, and your vehicle's parked out front, I doubt he'll return."

Kate declined the deputy's offer to come search the house again, explaining she had already had a second go at it and was convinced the cabin was clear.

"Clearin' it's about all I can do tonight, given that it's Christmas Eve," he said. "We're already short-handed, and I don't have our evidence tech scheduled until day after tomorrow. This ain't an emergency, so I can't justify bringin' him in to dust and collect whatever evidence is there. I'd advise you just leave it be 'til then and I'll send him over. Though I doubt it'll do much good," he added.

Leave it all alone? Leave the Christmas tree in the attic? No way. She wasn't going to let her philandering ex-husband spoil her last Christmas in her family cabin, and she wasn't going to let some random intruder do it either.

"Look, I'll leave the blankets and the rest of his makeshift campsite, but I'm not ruining my Christmas over this. I need that tree. Just send whoever in a couple of days to collect whatever evidence they can. Like you said, it probably won't help anyway."

Kate hung up, her insides groaning at the thought of another visit from the authorities. Her short, last Christmas in the cabin was quickly being derailed—*no, taken from her*—by these unplanned distractions. But this couldn't be helped. She needed them to investigate, and especially to dust for fingerprints, because she had another idea about who might be responsible. And it was someone infinitely more dangerous than a troublemaking teenager or random burglar.

Shoving down the fear this notion kindled, Kate marched back into the attic. Ignoring the area the intruder had made his own, she disassembled the tree, packing the lights and ornaments into an empty tub. Then she separated the tree into its two pieces, and began hauling it all downstairs.

10

She had grabbed the rifle. Again.
From a safe distance in the woods, hidden behind a hefty tree trunk for cover, his gloved hands gripped binoculars, pressing the eyepieces against his face. She was putting up the Christmas tree now, but earlier, through snow that had lightened to flurries, he watched her race down the stairs and duck behind the couch. She had popped up with the rifle seconds later, loaded it and raced back upstairs. Even though he had only managed a quick look at her face, it was long enough to make out the fear etched into it.

She was spooked. Again.

He sucked in a shivering breath. It was cold out here and he was already tired of standing in the snow. But he had to see. He had to know.

And what he knew was that she'd gone for the rifle twice in less than twenty-four hours. Which suggested Kate Palmer was a woman on the edge. Now it was just a matter of inching her closer and closer, until she was dangling precariously, ready to fall. Until it wouldn't take much to simply push her off the precipice.

Whether or not that was something he would have to do was entirely up to her.

11

It was as if the set of a Christmas movie had been staged in the cabin's living room. Kate had meticulously assembled the tree beside the stone hearth fireplace. Now its multicolored lights twinkled red, green, blue, and yellow beams that cheerfully bounced off the ornaments. There were fragile gold-and-red patterned globes, crystal icicles and silver bells. Mixed with these were homemade ornaments she and her siblings had made for her grandparents over the years—casts of handprints, baked-and-painted dough snowmen and Santas, and drawings of the Nativity scene taped onto colored cardboard frames.

The fire crackled heartily, the wood popping occasionally as sparks flew. The fire, candles she had lit around the room, and the tree provided the only illumination. Kate had pulled back the sheers on every window so she could watch the snow that was coming down hard again. She sat in the corner of the couch, taking it all in, slowly eating the beef and vegetable soup she had thrown together and her second roll dripping with butter.

The cabin's stereo was an old one with a turntable. Pop's Christmas records by Bing Crosby, Andy Williams, and Nat King Cole serenaded her, the perfect backdrop to the perfect Christmas vista.

Only it didn't feel perfect. Not by a long shot. Because this was the type of experience meant to be shared. For the first time, she questioned her decision to be there alone.

Maybe I should have gone to Mom and Dad's after all. She had been invited. And even though Brianna's and Shaun's families were going to be there, making it emotionally difficult, it might have been better to be around people. People that loved her unconditionally. They had even offered to join her at the cabin. But she had turned them down.

Thinking about that reminded her why it had been so important for her to come here. Alone.

Because I can't say goodbye to Erik and this cabin, not the way I need to, with other people around. And she wanted this to be a true goodbye. A never-look-back, get-on-with-your-life, good riddance kind of goodbye. Not to the cabin—that was something that would sting for a long time to come—but to the life partner she had so misjudged.

Kate scraped her bowl, downing the last spoonful of tender beef, corn, green beans, and rich, tomatoey broth. She put the bowl on the coffee table next to her phone. Her eyes flicked to its dark screen.

Don't.

A magnetic pull called to her fingers.

Don't.

She picked the phone up, ignoring the warning voice

inside. Even though she knew better, once again her will power was unable to beat back the cravings her jealousy and darker moments inspired.

In seconds, her phone displayed the latest photo of Erik and Miranda Palmer in full HD, umpteen-pixel, retina-display glory.

Erik and Miranda Palmer.

Holly had made her promise to delete and block Erik on Instagram after catching her sneak glimpses of his feed a few months ago. She had snatched the phone from Kate's hand and refused to give it back until Kate swore she would stop looking at it.

"*It's cruel and unusual punishment!*" Holly had barked. "*You're only making it worse for yourself. He's horrible for putting this out there, knowing what it could do to you, but you're the one choosing to be a victim by looking.*" Embarrassed at being caught in the act and knowing full well Holly was right, Kate had promised to never look at it again and clicked unfollow under Holly's watchful eye. Holly wasn't stupid. She made her do the same with Miranda's account, which Kate was ashamed to admit she had also been following.

Kate didn't violate vows. She believed in keeping her word.

Your word is your bond.

Pop had uttered that well-worn idiom so many times. And it had stuck. But she hadn't kept her word to Holly. She re-followed both Erik and Miranda after waiting long enough that Holly wouldn't ask. Kate still remembered how her stomach churned, a slippery heat crawling through her insides, the moment she pressed the digital button to do it, breaking her promise.

But keeping track of them had become more than a habit. It was a need. It fed something in her, and not something good. Still, at least once a day she tortured herself with photographs of the ecstatic newlyweds.

Mr. and Mrs. Erik Palmer.

While Kate struggled over breaking even her small promise to Holly, Erik had demonstrated he had no issue breaking his monumental vow of marriage. The ink on their divorce papers had barely dried before he declared his intention to marry the mistress. And not in some discreet way, protecting Kate's feelings.

No.

He did it for the world to see with an Instagram post of Miranda's hand on his, her black nail polish a striking contrast to the gleaming pear-shaped diamond ring and band mounted on her finger.

FINALLY MADE HER MINE. #FOREVER

Erik's post was short, simple, and absolutely crushing.

In their life *before*, his posts had been of her, or them, or places they were going or their little adventures in and out of the city. Art he found and loved. A new coffee joint he'd stumbled onto.

Now they were full of *her*. Miranda. With her striking jet-black hair with smooth curls and that twenty-five-year-old skin, blemish-free and decorated with an adorable smattering of freckles across the bridge of her nose and cheekbones. Miranda smiling. Miranda and Erik smiling together. A new piece of art they loved. Coffee at some new place that was *theirs*. Shots from all over Charleston where they lived now. Sunrises over the water, historic pastel-colored mansions, sailboats—it all made their life seem like a full-time vacation, which, Kate supposed, it was.

She didn't know much about Miranda Palmer. Except that Kate's internet searches revealed she was Miranda *Townsend* before she ran off with Erik, and that she was a self-declared trust-fund kid, as proudly announced in her Instagram bio.

Sunshine, stilettos and Erik for life. Trust fund makes living my best life possible. Sorry, not sorry.

"*Sorry, not sorry*"?

What kind of person writes something like that—makes that their mantra for the world to see?

And what did Erik see in that kind of person?

Could it have been the money? Sure, things had been tight for them financially, with the Nashville house and the cabin. She had taken out a second mortgage on the cabin to pay off the reverse mortgage Pop had on it when he died. There was equity there, enough to let her keep the Nashville house if she sold the cabin, but having both while she and Erik were together had made things tight.

Or was it something else? Age? She wasn't that much older than Miranda. Had he just grown bored? If he had, he had never given any hint of discontentment. Nothing suggesting he might be open to a way out. Even after twelve months of rehashing it in her mind, she couldn't come up with a single red flag. Which was why his leaving had been, and still was, such a shock.

The shift of her thoughts from Christmas to Erik left her feeling chilled, even though the fire still crackled and danced, its heat amply filling the space. This chill originated from Kate's center, something she had been unable to quash ever since Erik left. It wasn't always a bad thing. Sometimes if the chill grew cold enough, it would numb her. And numb was better than feeling, when all you ever felt was pain.

She hated that. That sometimes she had to go numb just to survive. That wasn't her personality before. Before Erik left, her friends would have described her as fun, happy, even bubbly. The life of the party. But the party was over, and now this half-life was all that was left.

He had hijacked her life. Her dreams. Even her personality, if she was honest.

How much longer was this going to go on?

How much longer was she going to let it?

Kate's gaze returned to the tree and the ornaments hanging from its branches. So many memories were wrapped up in each piece. She relived them all as she hung them one by one on the tree. Carefully. Lovingly. Wiping tears as she went. There was so much goodness here in this cabin. The very best of times. The very best of *her*.

Her eyes fell on the substantial stone mantel and the Bible that had belonged to her grandparents resting on it. She had insisted the Bible stay in the cabin when her family had selected sentimental items to take with them. Kate moved to the fireplace, its heat enveloping her.

The thick black book was well-worn, leather missing on spots along the edges. Her eyes grew wet remembering Pop's veined hands holding it open, reading to the whole family during one of his "lessons," or when reciting the passage in Luke about the birth of Jesus on Christmas Eve. She could almost hear his deep baritone voice recalling the angel's visit to Mary, the journey to Bethlehem and the birth in the stable.

She returned to the couch with the Bible, wrapped herself in a blanket and read the account out loud. The words were a balm to her soul, bringing back memories and reminding her of better days and what was important. Of what was still important. Of what couldn't be taken from her. Not by anyone.

Somewhere in her depths, something shifted. An ember sparked in her icy, chilled center. With tears rolling down her face, she could sense the ice melting, revealing something like...determination...beneath.

This cabin was her home. More so than the place in Germantown had been. Yes, she loved that house, and yes, she wanted to keep it. It was close to her business in the city, and close to the life she had—or thought she had—before Erik left. Holding on to it was holding on to what she had tried to build.

But now, here in this moment, it was so clear. She couldn't sell the cabin. No matter what.

If she kept it, though, it would mean selling the Germantown house. There was no other way to pay Erik his half of the equity in that place. It would also mean finding a cheaper place in Nashville she could afford on her salary—one she could pay for *and* keep paying the mortgage on the cabin. She would lose her Germantown community. She would lose her easy commute to work. And she would be forfeiting the satisfaction of keeping her dream house even though Erik had abandoned their dream.

I guess it comes down to which matters more.

And now she knew, that was the cabin. The legacy mattered more.

Yes, there would be losses, but it would also mean she was finally calling the shots. He didn't stay, he didn't choose her, and yet he was essentially still controlling her, forcing the sale of the cabin to satisfy what he was "owed." Not anymore.

I am going to do this.

Erik had trampled the marriage vows they had made. So she was going to make a new vow. To herself.

This cabin was going to remain in her family. A part of the Kincaid family legacy. And someday when she had a family of her own with a man who truly loved her the way she deserved to be loved, they would bring their children and their grandchildren here. And she would read the Christmas account to them from this Bible in front of this fire just like Pop had.

Kate clutched the worn book to her chest. For the first time in so very long, a peace settled over her. Her eyes moved to the tree, tracing it from its twinkling bottom all the way to the gold foil star topper that had been a hallmark of her childhood.

"I remember now, Pop and Mama K," she whispered. "I remember. And I promise—I vow—" she gripped the Bible even tighter, pressing it hard against herself, "to make this right. No matter what."

12

Kate woke on Christmas morning, still on the couch, toasty warm, wrapped in blankets. Brilliant white gleamed through the windows, the cloud-filtered sunlight reflecting off the fresh inches of snow outside.

She blinked and yawned, rolling over to check the fire, which had burned itself out during the night. She smiled. Another flame, however, was still burning brightly. Only this one was inside her.

Something was different today. And it wasn't just that she had gotten the best sleep she'd had in over a year. No, this was deeper.

"Merry Christmas to me," she said, and discovered she meant it without the slightest hint of sarcasm. She felt her mouth stretch into a grin, remembering sitting before the tree last night and reading the story of Christ's birth. This was His day, and she was going to celebrate and be thankful. She had spent enough time being the victim.

She offered a silent prayer, thanking God for the blessings in her life, for being her refuge during this time of struggle and for sending Christ into the world. For keeping His word. God was not one to ever break His vows.

Then she sat up, throwing off the blankets and planting her feet on the floor. If things were going to change, today was the perfect day to make a start.

Kate reached for her phone and opened up Instagram, intentionally making an effort not to look at the feed. Using the fictional account she had created to keep tabs on Erik and Miranda, she pulled up the accounts she was following, scrolled down to Erik's and with the single press of a forefinger on the screen, unfollowed him. This tiny physical gesture sparked the internal equivalent of a hundred cannon blasts. Liberation reigned in her, and she could almost hear bells of freedom clanging. Spurred on by the feeling, she scrolled to Miranda's account and unfollowed her as well.

For the first time since Erik had left, she felt free.

There was so much to do to change directions. So many people to call. Realtors, lawyers, loan officers...but it was Christmas. No one was working today, and rightfully so. It would have to wait. But first thing tomorrow, she would begin.

Kate hopped up, determined to whip up the best Christmas cinnamon French toast she had ever made. *For herself.* Then she would start making lists and budgets, and crack her laptop open to look for a new place in Nashville. *For herself.* She chuckled, feeling inspired.

Everything is going to be all right.

She must have said that to herself hundreds of times in the past twelve months. But this time, she actually believed it.

With a renewed sense of possibility she grabbed her cell to call her parents, wish them a Merry Christmas and share the good news.

13

Kate could barely contain her grin as she stood on Georgia and Rex's porch. Their place was about twice the size of hers and looked more like an Aspen chalet than a Great Smokies cabin. There was also a large shed and separate garage on the other side of their drive. Their family had money when they bought the property and hadn't spared it when building this getaway. They couldn't have known it would later become Georgia and Rex's primary residence, but it was a fortunate result because the two of them living year-round in a place as small as Kate's would've been tough.

Balancing an armful of goodies piled up to her chin, Kate used her elbow to knock awkwardly on the door and stepped back.

Georgia opened the door to the cabin, her smile wide. "I'm so glad you changed your mind, and wow," she said, reaching for the game boxes on top of Kate's stack, "you've got quite a load there." Kate stepped past her into the foyer, her arms still laden with heavy dishes of food—two aluminum pans and a red ceramic baking dish filled with a hot cherry strudel she had just pulled out of the oven.

"And Merry Christmas," Georgia called over her shoulder, before yelling, "Rex!" as she closed the front door. Rex appeared at the entrance to the hall leading into the rest of the cabin, heading straight for Kate. He stretched his hands toward the bottom dish to relieve her of it.

"Rex, no!" Kate exclaimed, turning her body to keep the dish out of his reach. He stepped back at the admonition, his shoulders dropping. "Sorry, Kate," he muttered, looking sheepish.

"No, it's okay. That one's just really hot. See? I have gloves on," she said, jiggling the handles she was holding in her gloved hands. "Would you mind getting the top two, though? They aren't hot."

"Oh. Okay, sure." He stood straighter now, all shades of embarrassment gone as he lifted the top two pans. He carried them into the enormous kitchen, decked out with marble countertops and sparkling stainless steel appliances, with Kate following right behind.

Rex's gentle soul was easily unsettled but just as easily set right again with a kind word and gracious explanation. Heaven help the person who didn't have that kind of patience with him, though, if Georgia found out. Kate had witnessed this truth firsthand when they were younger and some bullies from down the road had been giving Rex a hard time in his own front yard. Georgia had swooped in, threatening to take her softball bat to them, chasing them off. Georgia had hopped on her bike and, with Kate pedaling furiously to keep up, went straight to the boys' parents, telling on them without a second thought. Georgia's fierce protection of Rex was something Kate loved about her. And it was mutual; Rex was just as loyal to his sister.

If only Erik had been that loyal.

She mentally slapped at the wistful thought.

This is a new beginning. No more of that.

Taking a deep breath, she swept the notion away like dust out a door.

"I wasn't expecting all this," Georgia said, waving her arms over the three pans. She eyed the clear lid on the ceramic bakeware. "Cherry strudel?" Her eyes twinkled as Rex leaned over her shoulder. She lifted the lid, releasing the tangy, sweet aroma of cherries and brown sugar.

Rex smiled at Kate, and she grinned back. "I didn't forget it was your favorite thing Mama K used to make," she said, patting Rex's shoulder. "There's sweet potato casserole and fresh-baked rolls too—from scratch," she added when Georgia side-eyed her dubiously. "I had the cleaners stock the fridge with the ingredients for my go-to Christmas dishes, just in case I felt like cooking."

She had only done that as a matter of routine. She hadn't expected to actually feel like cooking any of it. But her newfound perspective had reenergized her, yanking her out of her depression overnight.

"What do you think of the tree, Kate?" Rex asked, walking into their living room where a giant live tree towered at least twelve feet high. Blue and silver ornaments filled its branches, and thick-fringed silver garland wound from top to bottom. Beside the tree a fire blazed in the oversized fireplace with a raised stone hearth large enough to sit on.

"I love it," Kate answered.

Rex reached for one of the ornaments and adjusted it.

While he busied himself with that, Kate sidled up to Georgia beside the large kitchen island made of black-and-white swirled marble.

"You know, you surprise me, Kate Palmer," Georgia started. "Yesterday you weren't even up for coming over. I never imagined you'd be up for Christmas cooking."

"Hey, you brought Battleship™?" Rex exclaimed. He had moved to where Georgia had stacked the game boxes on their coffee table, a beautiful piece made of tree trunk cut lengthwise, polished to a smooth finish and covered with a glass top.

"Yep," answered Kate. "I remember you played that with Pop. I didn't know if you had one."

"This is great," he said, holding the box in his hands like a long-lost treasure he discovered.

"We've got one too, but he'll love playing Pop's game," Georgia said. "They used to play all the time, you know." She put the pan of sweet potato casserole in the oven to warm. "If cooking's therapeutic for you, you're welcome to come over here the rest of the week and work out your demons."

"It's not that," Kate said, biting her bottom lip, the corners of her mouth pulling up in anticipation. "I took a big step today. I blocked Erik's Instagram account."

Georgia's eyebrows rose. "You did?"

Kate nodded. "I don't need that in my life anymore. Following him. Following her—oh, I blocked her too. *Miranda.*" Kate's insides dipped a little at the venom still in her voice when she said that woman's name. She may have deleted the social media accounts, but she had a long way to go.

"Deleting those accounts is a big step," Georgia said.

"I was checking them way too often, keeping up with

where they were going, what they were doing, what they looked like. Erik didn't even look like the same person. It's as if he's changed everything about him. His beard is all grown out and...well, it doesn't matter. And that's not all." She braced herself for Georgia's reaction. "I decided I'm keeping the cabin."

Georgia's mouth dropped open. Then one corner pulled up into a half-smile. "You're what?" she asked, tilting her ear toward Kate as though she heard her incorrectly.

Kate nodded. "I'm keeping the cabin. I'm not selling."

Georgia's eyes widened. "Seriously?"

"Seriously. I'll sell the place in town. I don't want to, but I can't keep both mortgages. I'll have to get something small in Nashville, and probably out of the way, but—"

Before she could finish, Georgia had gathered her into a smothering hug. "Kate, that's amazing news." After several seconds and possibly a couple of broken ribs, she pulled back to look Kate in the eye. "Oh, I can't believe it," she squealed, pulling Kate to her again.

Rex's timid voice piped in. "Are you really going to stay, Kate?"

She hadn't realized he was listening. She extracted herself from Georgia's grip and walked over to Rex, taking his hand. "I am. It's the right thing to do. I can't let Pop and Mama K's place go."

A vibrant pink flushed Rex's cheeks. He stood there, seemingly uncertain of what to do. It wasn't a secret that he had harbored a bit of a crush on Kate since they were kids. She settled it for him by enveloping him in a hug.

"That's really good news, Rex," Georgia said, joining them, and patting her brother's shoulder encouragingly.

He nodded in confirmation, still a little abashed. "It's good news."

"One of the worst things about selling the cabin was losing the two of you as neighbors," Kate said, giving him a gentle punch in the arm. "I didn't like the thought of not seeing you anymore."

"Well," Georgia started, cracking another smile, "if that's not a Christmas gift, I don't know what is. What do you guys say we set the table, pop that turkey out of the oven and get this celebration started?"

Her belly full, Kate sat, or rather laid, on the U-shaped couch facing Georgia's stone fireplace. Between the food she brought and Georgia's turkey, corn casserole, mashed potatoes, and bacon-sprinkled green beans, she probably weighed twenty pounds more than when she arrived. She would be miserable if she weren't so content.

They had played three rounds of Battleship™, with Rex besting her in two out of three. Now he was curled up in his favorite overstuffed chair, lost in a Western novel Georgia had given him that morning. Kate watched him and felt a smile leak onto her face. Being here, with these two, in this place, made things feel almost normal.

She had always loved this room with its high ceiling and transverse rough-hewn beams, expansive panoramic windows covering the front and right sides, and the multiple varieties of stained woods comprising the walls, trim, and doors.

Kate sipped her hot chocolate, staring out those windows

into the woods. She remembered once, as a teen, looking out and seeing a black bear cub wander out of the trees. The mother had quickly appeared, chasing her little one back into the cover of the woods.

It made her think about other things that might be hiding in the cover of those woods. Things hiding in her own cabin.

"Georgia?" Kate asked.

"Hmm?" Georgia replied, pulling away from her own mug.

"I know it's not like you can see my place from here, but have you seen anyone wandering around in the general area? Somebody that shouldn't be there?"

"Is this about the items missing from the cabin? Rex told me about that after he came home yesterday."

"No. Not that. At least, I don't know if it's connected to that." Noticing Georgia's confused expression, Kate realized she wasn't making any sense. "The deputies think that trespassing teenagers or possibly a frustrated burglar were responsible for the missing items and things moved around in the cabin."

"Well, that makes sense."

"Except, the things they moved around and what they took...it was almost as if the goal was to unnerve me. Like they knew what would bother me most."

"What are you trying to say?" Georgia asked.

Kate exhaled, knowing how stupid this was going to sound. But she had to bounce it off someone. "Well...I wondered if it might be...well...Erik." She felt her cheeks redden with heat.

Georgia's posture straightened. "Erik? Why would he do that? Isn't he on the coast somewhere?"

"Charleston," Kate clarified.

"Yeah, so how would he take them? And even if he could, why would he?"

"I don't know. To get under my skin? To punish me for not selling sooner? I've been dragging my feet on this for a while, so he hasn't gotten his share of the money."

"You said his wife was rich. I just don't see the benefit for him. Seems pretty implausible."

"So does dumping your wife by leaving a letter stuck in a Christmas tree. I don't think of him as the most rational person."

Georgia rocked her head back and forth. "That's fair," she conceded.

"I also thought of another possibility." Kate paused, watching her friend's face for her reaction. "What about Martin Bleeker?"

"Wait...is that...is that the guy that you got the restraining order against?"

Kate nodded. "I haven't seen or heard from him since the order went into effect two years ago. But he did break into our house in Nashville before that, so, I thought maybe he did the same thing at the cabin. Maybe took a few mementos the way he took my hairbrush back then."

"I guess it's possible," Georgia said, biting her lip. "It sounds more plausible than Erik breaking in there."

"The thing is...I found a makeshift bedroom in my attic."

Georgia's face contorted. "You found *what* in your attic?"

The lines of concern etched into Georgia's face deepened as Kate described the scene she discovered when she went looking for the Christmas tree. "Someone stacked a bunch of storage tubs and boxes, creating their own little room. They even put the tree up in the corner."

Georgia set her mug on an end table, closed her eyes, then opened them, apparently having a hard time digesting what Kate was saying. "So someone is *living* in your attic?"

"Living...was living...I'm not sure. They didn't leave much behind. And unless they put that tree up years ago, it suggests they were there fairly recently. But they aren't there now. I searched the cabin again. No one else was there."

Georgia expelled a concerned sigh. "I don't like this."

"The more I think about it," Kate said, "the more it seems like something Bleeker would do. What if he couldn't be near me in the city so he came out here instead? He knew about the cabin. We talked about it one time when I was working at his house."

Georgia's visage darkened. "That's a pretty scary notion, Kate. And whether it's Bleeker or not, how can you be sure they're gone? Maybe you should stay with us. We wouldn't mind and we have the room."

Kate shook her head. "If I'm not letting Erik run me out of there by making me sell the cabin, I'm sure not letting some unknown trespasser do it. Or Bleeker." She hoped she sounded braver than she felt. Because the thought of Bleeker being in that attic put goosebumps on her arms beneath her wooly sweater sleeves. "Whoever it was will have seen my car if they're still around. They'll have seen me inside. They won't come back in."

"First, you can't know that. Second, did you tell the sheriff's office about it?" Georgia asked.

"I did, but not about Bleeker specifically. The deputies are coming over tomorrow to check it out, and I'll share my thoughts then. Even when I do tell them about Bleeker, I don't think it'll make a difference. I mean, what are they going to find that will change anything? I can't prove it was Bleeker."

"You never know. Fingerprints, maybe? Something you missed? Regardless, I think you're going to have to hire a management company to keep an eye on the place while you're gone throughout the year. Think about it. When you leave later this week, whoever *was* there could just come back then." Georgia's eyes widened. "They could be watching your place now. Watching you. Your comings and goings. What if they decide to break in one night?"

"You're not making this better."

"I'm not trying to. I'm trying to make sure you're safe," Georgia countered, pulling a swath of dark hair behind one shoulder.

The image of Pop's rifle resolved in Kate's mind. "I'm fine. I can protect myself. You don't need to worry."

"You know, this isn't the same place it was when your grandparents lived here. It's changed. There's more tourism. More people passing through. Donovan's Mercantile was robbed a couple of months ago."

Donovan's was a local family business that had been around forever. It was essentially a modern-day version of a general store, housed in a rustic wood-slat building, replete with swept hardwood floors and glass candy jars on the counter. It sold everything from groceries to gardening supplies to any caliber ammunition you might need in these woods. She knew the Donovan family well. Kate's stomach dropped at the thought of one of them being injured. "Was everyone okay?"

Georgia nodded. "They took the cash at gunpoint and

raced out of there. Nobody was hurt. I'm just saying that the Bloodroot Ridge of your grandparents' days doesn't exist anymore, and you should know that if you're keeping the cabin. You'll need to take proper precautions. Especially since someone's clearly already taken a liking to the place."

"I'll look into it," Kate said, and she meant it. If she really was taking this place on, she would need to keep it up properly and protect her investment. "Although I think having renters there should help in keeping the vagrants away," she added.

"Renters?" Georgia's tone drew up half a step. "You're really going to rent the place out to tourists? Your grandparents would have hated that."

"They would have hated me selling it even more. And hopefully, it won't be forever. But in the beginning, I'm going to need the cash if I'm going to pay for two places."

Georgia squeezed Kate's arm. "I get it. Do what you have to. I'm just glad you're not leaving us."

"Me too," Kate said, and hugged her friend.

"Just be careful over there, okay? Promise?" Georgia asked, her eyes pleading.

Kate squeezed her friend's hand. "I promise."

14

Back in her own cabin, Kate lay in bed, drifting in and out of sleep as the wind howled outside. She had returned from Georgia's around eleven, completely exhausted. After depositing the leftovers in the fridge, she changed, then crawled under the covers. Now she burrowed deeper, frustrated that despite how tired she was, sleep eluded her.

Probably all the talk about intruders and robberies. In hindsight, it really hadn't been the kind of thing to discuss on Christmas, especially on an evening she had been enjoying so much prior to bringing it up. But she had felt a responsibility to share the information. Georgia and Rex's place wasn't that far away. If someone was trespassing on her property, chances were they were trespassing on the Cranes' property too. They needed to know so they could be vigilant. She didn't want them in danger any more than she wanted to be in danger herself.

Kate rolled over and stared at the old-fashioned brass

chandelier hung over the bed. Like everything else, it had been there as long as she could remember. Kate's mind began to wander, considering options for updating the place. She would want to keep much of it the same for sentimentality's sake. But she also wanted to make it her own, which meant utilizing her interior design talents to blend the old and new into something uniquely hers. If she wanted to attract renters at a high-end rate, there would need to be some changes.

A makeover within a modest budget would be necessary—new countertops, plush throws and swivel rockers by the fire...Anything she wanted to keep that didn't fit with the new decor—the handmade knit throws, needlepoint pillows, and framed photos—she could store and bring back out when she visited the cabin...

Her mind slowed as the possibilities blurred, the warmth of the bed and the contentment from the day working together to lull her to sleep.

Bang!

Kate shot up, her heart slamming in her chest, her eyes and ears laser-focused down the hall—the direction she thought the sound had originated from. Several quiet moments passed, and she almost convinced herself she must have imagined the noise when it came again.

Bang! Bang!

A burst of adrenaline flushed Kate's system, all her nerve-endings seeming to fire at once. Someone was hammering on the front door. Her mind instantly went to the rifle hidden beneath the bed. She uttered a prayer for protection as she slid out, dropped to her knees and withdrew the weapon from its hiding place beneath a spare blanket. Her eyes cut to her phone charging on the nightstand. She reached up and clicked the power button. The home screen came up.

No messages. Whoever was at the door, it wasn't Georgia or Rex trying to get ahold of her.

Bang! Bang! The hammering was hard and demanding but also oddly disjointed, with long stretches of cryptic silence between each instance—at least twenty or thirty seconds since the last one.

She shoved the phone in the pocket of her flannel pajamas and rose, walking with the rifle in front of her, ready to fire.

Please, Lord, don't let me have to fire.

"Who's there?" No reply came. "I'm warning you! Answer me! Who's there?"

Kate's mind raced. *Should I call the sheriff? But what if it's just Rex and he's not answering because he can't hear me?* The last thing she wanted was to cause him trouble or call the sheriff out again unnecessarily. *But if it's not Rex...*

She had made her way to the living room and now stood at the bottom of the stairs. There hadn't been any more banging since she left the bedroom.

"I mean it! I'll call the sheriff! Who's there?"

Again, no one answered.

She was desperate to look through the peephole. But caution told her that standing directly in front of the door when the unknown person on the other side might be armed wasn't exactly wise. She was holding a rifle aimed directly at the door. What if they were too?

What if it's whoever was in the attic, returning to reclaim their place?

What if it's Bleeker?

Bleeker had never threatened *her*. His behavior had been creepy—following her around Nashville, turning up in restaurants she went to and causing scenes, breaking into her home...But all of that culminated in letters professing his love for her and his belief that she secretly loved him too. The only threats he made were in those letters, directed against anyone who might try to stop them from being together.

So if it was Bleeker at the door, he probably wasn't pointing a gun at the door waiting to blow her away. Although, a lot had changed since that letter. She had rejected him. She had gotten a restraining order, publicly humiliating him.

So maybe she shouldn't be so quick to assume he wouldn't want to hurt her now. In fact, what if revenge, not love, was what he sought?

Kate realized there hadn't been any more knocking. It had been, what, thirty seconds? A minute?

Had they gone? Or were they just lulling her into a sense of security. Making her believe the danger had passed.

She stepped to the window to the left of the door that overlooked the porch and sucked in a wavering breath.

There was no banging. No anything.

With her back against the thick wood that made up the cabin's wall, she reached one hand out and pulled back the drapes just enough to create a slit that would allow her to get a look at whoever was there.

Moving slowly, she leaned in, putting one eye just inside the slit until she could see the space in front of the door.

Overwhelming relief and raw worry crashed against each other in her gut.

The porch was empty. Whoever had been there was gone.

15

The rest of the night was an exhausting stretch of struggling to stay awake on the couch, drinking coffee, falling asleep anyway, then jerking awake at the slightest sound. One hand remained ready on the rifle, the other curled around her phone.

She hadn't called a soul about...well, whatever that was. It was after midnight when it happened, and she didn't want to wake Georgia and Rex or spoil what had been a great Christmas.

She probably should have called the sheriff's office, but what would she tell them? That someone had banged on her door? And then left? Even though they had knocked repeatedly—and in that creepy way of waiting an extended period between insistently banging—it wasn't exactly a crime. It wasn't even menacing, actually. Not by itself. But taken together with the time of night, and the missing and disturbed items, *and* the campsite in the attic, it just felt very, very wrong.

The lights were all on, and she had the fire going. If anyone was watching the cabin, they would know she was up and ready for them. She checked her phone for the umpteenth time.

3:17 a.m.

The deputies would be there by nine in the morning. At least that's what they told her on Christmas Eve. She could make it until nine.

I can make it.

Kate stopped on the sidewalk, turning to look at her husband. "I can't believe you. I just don't even know who you are anymore," she said, her eyes on Erik, the blue pools of her irises full of disbelief.

"What? I can't help how I feel," he replied unashamedly.

"You're going to stand there and tell me you honestly believe those tacos we just ate are better than the ones at Ramon's Truck."

Erik shrugged. "I don't know what to tell you. My stomach doesn't lie."

Kate snorted. "We've been eating at Ramon's Truck for three years. You insisted on having your birthday there. And now you're just willing to turn your back on all that?"

Erik grinned through his auburn stubble and slung an arm around Kate as he pulled her onward, making their way down the sidewalk in the West End of Nashville. Tradition held that Friday night was "new restaurant night," and tonight they had opted for The Caliente Grill.

"Okay, *you* tell me that you honestly didn't think those were the best tacos you've ever had, and I'll reconsider."

"*Honestly*, Ramon's are better," Kate insisted. "They're smothered in cheese and these were—"

Erik grabbed her around the waist and kissed the back of her neck. "You are such a liar!" He dug his fingers into her waist, right where he knew she was ticklish. "Liar!"

This part of Nashville was bustling at nine on a Friday night, and Kate laughed so loudly, heads turned on the sidewalk around them. "Stop, okay, stop," she chuckled, shoving his hands away. "Fine. Fine! They were better!"

"Ha!" he belted out, pulling her back to him and properly kissing her before turning her loose. "I knew it."

She wanted to look annoyed, to continue to egg him on, but she couldn't help grinning at the ridiculous expression on his face. The one that said he knew he had bested her. "Okay," she conceded, working hard to sound at least a little miffed. "You knew it." Straightening her shoulders, she quickly rallied. "But come on, it's Ramon. *Ramon!* He's our friend—"

"I'm not gonna *tell* him, Kate," he said, holding his hand out to her. She slipped her fingers between his as they started walking. "It'll be our secret. And besides, just because I like the tacos better doesn't mean I like the place better. You still can't beat the picnic tables at Ramon's."

"Exactly."

"Oh, hey. Look at this." His hand tugged on hers as he stopped in front of a closed shop, its display window filled with an array of tiny outfits in pinks, blues and yellows. Silk daffodils covered the floor and brightly-colored balloons on sticks were arranged like trees on either side of a sign that said, "Springtime is in the Air." He tapped his finger on the glass, indicating a faint blue cotton jumper with embroidered rabbits on the chest. "I mean...come on."

Kate tapped the glass in front of the pink twin of the jumper. "I'm partial to that one." She turned to him, expecting to see him shaking his head in disagreement, but his dark brown eyes were watching her intently.

"What?" she asked.

"I was just thinking how lucky any child of ours will be if they even look a little like you."

Embarrassment flushed her face with heat, and she chortled softly.

"I'm serious," he said.

She cocked her head, as the corner of her mouth turned up. She wasn't comfortable with direct compliments. Not even from him. "You're being cheesy."

He grabbed her hand. "I thought you *loved* cheese."

"When it's on tacos," she said, leaning her head into his shoulder.

"Well, you better get used to it. Because I'm not changing anytime soon."

A loud sob erupted from Kate, cruelly yanking her out of her memory and her restless sleep on the couch.

She blinked. Light peeked out from the edges of the drawn drapes. Morning had finally come. Her cheeks were wet, and she swiped at them, anger flaring. She hadn't had that stupid dream in so long.

That night happened during the April before Erik left. Eight months later he was gone. The memory was a perfect example of why she had been so blindsided by Erik leaving her. Sure, they had some rough patches in the months that had followed, including some financial issues when she lost a few clients and a scare with the state psychiatry board when a patient filed a complaint against Erik. The decision to hold off on kids for one more year because of all those issues had been a mutual one. In her mind, they had navigated the difficult season just fine, looking ahead toward fulfilling their dreams. But she must have been wrong, because he left and took with him those dreams of a life together and children who would inherit the best parts of both of them.

She closed her eyes. *Lord, please. Just help me let go. Just help me forget. It's too painful. I don't want to go there anymore.*

She took a deep breath that filled her whole belly, slowly exhaled, then stood. Shuffling into the kitchen, she brewed another cup of coffee, chugged a few gulps, then headed to the shower.

That was then. This is now.
And now it's time for me to move forward.
Starting with reclaiming what's mine.

16

When Deputy Lyle and his partner, Deputy Cawthorne, arrived a little after nine, Kate was ready for them. Coffee and the shower had helped to shake off the weariness after a night of troubled sleep, but the terror she had felt waking to the banging on her door was still fresh. Standing in her living room, Kate described the late-night intrusion in detail while they listened patiently, taking notes. Unlike last time, this new development seemed to spark serious concern.

"Maybe you'd better think about staying elsewhere until we get a better handle on what's goin' on here," Deputy Lyle suggested, rubbing his bearded chin with one hand.

"I actually have some thoughts about what's going on. Or at least, who might be behind it," Kate offered, then told them about Martin Bleeker.

"We'll have someone get a hold of Metro Nashville Police and check that out, try to verify Bleeker's whereabouts," said Deputy Lyle. He nodded at Deputy Cawthorne, who turned away, using her radio to call in about the situation. "I sure wish you'd explained more about last night before we got here, though," he said, grimacing. "We could've done a better job of checking for footprints in the snow before pulling into the drive and walking all over them."

"There were footprints there last night," Kate said, and pulled out her phone to show him photos. "There was only a dusting on the porch, but you can see where the snow's been disturbed." She pointed at the photo. "See how the prints lead down the steps and off to the right of the drive, toward the woods? I didn't want to go out to look, so I couldn't check out beyond that."

"Smart not to. Give me a minute." He explained to Deputy Cawthorne what he was going to do and opened the front door. "When was the last time you walked out here?" he asked Kate.

"Around eleven last night, when I got back from my friends' place—you know, the Cranes, right down the road?"

"Yeah, I know them."

"So, some of those footprints are probably mine. But I would have gone to and from my car," she pointed directly ahead, "not that way," she finished, thumbing toward the woods to the right.

Deputy Lyle took several photos of the porch, the drive, and the area around the front of the cabin. Careful not to step on existing prints, he moved toward the woods, snapped more photos, then came back to Kate.

"It's been snowing pretty good on and off over the last couple of days, so it's hard to tell when these were made. But it does look like someone came in and out of the woods, headed for your front door. Do you know anything about that?"

Rex had walked over a couple of times. "Possibly. Rex Crane did walk over on the night of the twenty-third and on Christmas Eve. He could've made those then. You'd have to ask him."

"The tire tracks in your drive aren't goin' to be much help, between being run over by other tracks and new snow. But just to cover our bases, did anyone else drive in here yesterday?"

"No. But Georgia Crane drove up here on Christmas Eve morning."

"And you're sure it wasn't one of them banging on your door last night?"

"No. They would have called or texted. I haven't heard from them at all."

"Okay, so, the best we can probably hope for is following those," he pointed to the footprints leading into the woods, "to see where they come out. But I can almost guarantee they won't continue much past the tree line. With all that tree canopy and brush cover, snow doesn't pile up the same way it does out in the open. We'll check it before we leave, though, just in case."

Kate nodded. She hadn't expected they would find much evidence outside. It was the inside she was more concerned with.

As if he had read her mind, Deputy Lyle said, "What do you say we go check out this makeshift campsite somebody set up in your attic."

The makeshift campsite was gone.

All of it. The blankets. The flashlight. The boxes had even been moved around so that any trace of a partitioned section was gone.

A rushing filled Kate's ears as disbelief flooded her. "Look!" she exclaimed, pulling her phone out. "See? I took photos! Someone was clearly staying here." She handed the phone over while they scrolled through the shots. She turned in circles, her arms outstretched. "It was all here. I don't know what happened."

"Has anyone been in the house with you?" Deputy Lyle asked.

"Not since I found all that stuff."

"What about after that?"

"No. Just me. Then I was gone Christmas afternoon and evening, like I said before. Maybe someone came in then..." Her voice trailed off as her thoughts churned.

If someone felt the need to remove this stuff now, then this is recent. Not something from years ago. She wrapped her arms around herself as disbelief turned to fear, crawling up her spine like a spider. Someone had been—was still—coming into the cabin. And sometime between Christmas Eve and this morning they had broken in and erased all evidence of their presence.

Why? Why risk coming back?

It was just a bunch of blankets. Boxes and storage tubs.

Fingerprints.

"I think we'd better get an evidence team in here to dust, just in case," Deputy Lyle said. "If they came back to clean up, it's looking less and less like a vagrant."

And more and more like someone was here on purpose. Like Bleeker.

"There'll be fingerprints everywhere," Kate said. "My whole family and movers were up here after my grandfather died, sorting through things."

"Still. We might get lucky. Especially if it is this Bleeker guy. If we manage to find a print that's his, that'll shed a lot of light on what's going on. Of course, if he came up here because of prints, chances are he wiped everything down." He nodded at Deputy Cawthorne who initiated another call on her radio. Deputy Lyle turned back to Kate, drawing his lips into a thin line before speaking. "Is there any possibility that the banging on the door last night and this," he wagged a finger at the space, "are related?"

Kate felt her forehead wrinkle. "What are you thinking?"

"Like maybe two people working together? One distracting you so the other could get into the attic and take the stuff out the back?"

That was a terrifying proposition. Why would any two people work together to essentially stalk her in this cabin? What could they possibly hope to gain?

Unless terrorizing me is the whole point.

Which once again, sounded like Bleeker. Maybe he had brought a friend.

Deputy Cawthorne stepped closer. "They'll send someone with the evidence team over within the hour," she told them.

"Look, if you're right about the front door being a distraction," Kate said, "then whoever cleaned out the attic would have had to leave through the back of the cabin, because I was blocking the front door."

"How many back doors are there?" Deputy Lyle asked.

"Just one. In the sitting room off the master suite." *My room. Which meant if someone was already upstairs when the banging started...they could have walked right past me, lying asleep in bed, to get there.*

Her heart thrumming, Kate stepped to the attic window, both deputies right behind her.

Leading away from the back of the cabin, straight into the woods behind it, was a clearly discernible set of tracks.

Kate sat on the floor of the attic, staring out the window and taking in its wide view of the backyard clearing and woodland expanse beyond. She held a blanket around her shoulders with one hand and a mug of tea in the other, finding the heat and aroma of the black tea leaves mixed with orange peel rather comforting.

At nearly three o'clock, the evidence technician had finally come and gone. According to him, it had been a pretty unsuccessful trip. His dusting turned up lots of prints from what appeared to be lots of different people, mostly unusable partials and somewhat degraded.

Not surprising when you consider how long Pop and Mama K had lived there and how many people had been in that attic moving things around over the years.

Also not surprising was that the storage boxes and tubs used to cordon off the private area—as shown in Kate's photos—had been wiped clean. No prints at all on those. And likely why the only prints on the attic doorknob were Kate's.

So it looked like whoever came back for their stuff *did* do it to avoid being identified, or at least that was part of their motivation.

The tech did try dusting some of the tree ornaments, but got nothing. Kate apologized for having moved them, but he said the surfaces weren't conducive to prints anyway, and it was unlikely they would have helped. In the end, the tech warned Kate not to expect much. In most cases like this, they didn't get a useful match. But they would run the prints he had managed to lift against Bleeker's prints and through the system and let her know what they found.

Besides the prints, they hadn't come up with any other physical evidence. She and the deputies had searched the attic area but came up empty. The squatter hadn't left so much as a piece of trash behind. The tracks outside hadn't led to anything useful either. Like Deputy Lyle had suspected, both the ones behind the house and to the side had petered out in the woods, given all the cover and undergrowth, so whoever had made them and wherever they had gone remained a mystery.

Kate wasn't a fool. She knew this investigation would probably stall out—unless Bleeker's name popped up in the fingerprint search. Otherwise, this wasn't a case that would warrant continuing effort. No real damage had been done, so there wasn't much at stake. Somebody had definitely scared her, but they hadn't hurt her.

There was something interesting about the tracks at the front of the cabin, though. Apparently, multiple sets of tracks led to and from the porch, not just one. But they crossed over each other and jumbled together, making it hard to tell which steps were from which path. And because of the continuing snowfall, it was hard to tell when each was made.

Kate had a pretty good idea how some of the tracks had ended up there, though. One call to Rex confirmed he had traveled in that general direction when he walked over on Christmas Eve afternoon, though he couldn't say exactly where he'd come out. So any of them could have been his and not from the mystery knocker at all. Which meant they were useless as a clue.

Deputy Lyle had tried to console her, suggesting that it could still have been a vagrant with a record who wanted to come back and wipe the place down. When she'd questioned why he hadn't just come and gone while she was at Georgia's, Deputy Lyle suggested maybe she'd come home in the middle of the act, and he'd hidden out of sight until he could slip out.

"Why not just go out the front then, while I was in bed?" she had asked him.

"Maybe he was trapped in your room and was too afraid you'd hear him when he moved. So he needed the distraction at the front door to get you out of there. He brought a buddy with him in case he needed help, and, I don't know, texted him to get him to bang on the door."

It was a lot of speculation on his part, but even so, the thought of someone hiding in her bedroom while she'd gotten in bed and gone to sleep hadn't gone over well. She didn't like that possibility. She didn't like any of the possibilities. She just wanted whoever it was to stay away, leave her alone, and let her get on with her life. She took another sip of tea, the brew warming her insides as she watched a squirrel bound up a tree.

This is ridiculous, she told herself. *You're not getting anywhere sitting here.*

She had thought it might help her work through things,

looking out at the same view her squatter had. But all she could think of was Bleeker and the danger he posed.

Bleeker had seemed harmless enough when she took him on as a client a few years ago. He was in his forties, divorced, and looking to update his Nashville home to reflect a more stream-lined, modern style. He told her someone—he conveniently couldn't remember who—had recommended Kate. But Bleeker was a real estate agent dealing in high-end properties who knew a lot of people, so that wasn't a red flag. He was unassuming, well-groomed, and had a gentle disposition that made you trust him right off the bat. At least Kate had.

Boy, had that been a mistake.

It didn't take long for Kate to pick up on something being...off. He started making overly enthusiastic comments about looking forward to seeing her and anticipating their next appointments. Then he started showing up wherever she was. Having lunch. Out with friends. Shopping. When he started leaving notes on her car, she fired him, and then it got ugly. He broke into her house. Stole a few personal items. Then he started sending the letters threatening Erik, or anyone else who got in the way of their "love." That's when she got the restraining order.

The last time she saw him was the day of the court hearing. After that, he just disappeared, like he'd never entered her world at all. That was two years ago.

What if he had found a way to stay in my world?

Whatever the case, this wasn't working. She was just wasting time. Time better spent on developing her new plan. She had a lot of research to do if she was going to keep the cabin. She had to find somewhere to live, and finding something affordable *and* within a reasonable commute was going to be daunting, if not nearly impossible. She also needed to take the cabin off the market and find someone to list the Germantown place.

Of course, it was the day after Christmas. No one was going to be working. But she could start making lists and at least begin the internet research before Rex and Georgia came over for dinner.

Something else she needed to get started on.

"All right," she told herself, downing the last of the tea and standing. "Time to get moving." She put her free hand on a corner of one of the tubs to push herself up and the whole thing turned over, throwing her off balance so that she dropped the mug and landed hard on her side.

"Ugh," Kate groaned, pushing up off the floor, grateful she had drained the mug first, or tea would have been all down her front. She righted the tub, one of the few that was nearly empty—which was why it hadn't held her weight—then turned in a circle, looking for the mug. It wasn't anywhere.

Then Kate spotted the long, open area along the entire back wall where the plywood floor stopped and the ceiling joists were exposed. She walked over to it, and sure enough, the mug had skidded into one of the insulation-filled spaces, lying half-buried in the fluffy stuff. Kate picked up the mug, dusted it off, and an idea struck.

She and the deputies had done a decent job of looking through the space, even moving boxes and tubs around, and checking under them. She even thought she remembered Deputy Cawthorne walking this same route, looking over into the spaces.

But had she really searched them?

After running downstairs to grab a set of dishwashing

gloves, she started at one end of the attic and worked her way along the edge, getting on her knees to dig through the mounds of fiberglass insulation in each box-like section created by the joists.

From a section just before the window, she pulled a ballpoint pen from a cottony pile lying just out of view, under the edge of the plywood. It was one of Pop's old pens, advertising a construction company he had owned in the 1980s. There was no telling how long that thing had been down there.

She kept moving, examining each space, pulling the fluff from as far beneath the plywood as she could reach, finding nothing other than some mouse droppings and some kind of nest an animal had fashioned out of straw-like material it had brought in from who-knew-where. Then she reached the area across from where the Christmas tree had stood, and saw the corner of what looked like a piece of paper in a narrow gap between the fluff and one of the joists. The paper was the same color as the insulation, making it practically invisible unless you were *really* looking.

Kate gently pulled it from its resting place. It was only a few inches wide and long, and folded in half. She casually unfolded it, expecting it would be another trivial relic from her grandparents' past, like the pen. But as she read it, a sudden weakness consumed her, her hands shaking and lightheadedness breaking over her as if all the air had been sucked out of the room.

Then the doorbell rang.

17

Kate bounded down the stairs, headed for the front door. Still reeling from the discovery in the attic, her mind now spun wildly with the possibilities of who would just show up. Unannounced. Something about it didn't bode well.

Had the deputies returned to update her in person without calling first because they had bad news? Did that mean some of the prints were a match for Bleeker?

The proposition made her more weak in the knees than she already was, and she nearly tripped over the last stair step. But as she righted herself, she remembered that the evidence tech said it would be at least a day or two before the fingerprint results came back. They had to send them off for processing, and the Christmas holiday might mean even more delays.

So it couldn't be that.

She looked through the peephole. A man she had never

seen before stood on the porch, clad in a sharp wool coat and dress shoes unsuited for the snow.

"Who is it?" she called out, still eyeing him through the peephole.

"Hi," he answered in a pleasant tone, his smile revealing glaringly white teeth. The distortion of the peephole's fisheye lens made his smile more jarring than friendly. Taking in his clean-shaven face, she guessed he was in his late-thirties. "I'm Carl Norton, of Norton Realtors out of Maryville." Maryville was the nearest town, twenty-five minutes away from Bloodroot Ridge. He held a business card up. "I'm here to speak with you about the sale of your cabin? I understand you're putting it on the market and—"

At the mention of the sale, Kate jerked the door partially open, remaining half-hidden behind it. "Sorry, how did you know I was considering that?"

He blinked, cocking his head slightly. "Um, your friend—Georgia Crane—we know each other," he answered. "She told me you were selling and suggested I stop by. She didn't feel right about sharing your cell number, so, I thought I'd come myself to—"

"It's the day after Christmas. Still part of the holiday. I'm surprised you'd come today," Kate said, injecting the slightest hint of annoyance into her tone. Something about his overeager approach, like a vulture wanting to claim the roadkill first, bothered her.

"Yes, well, early bird, and all that," he replied confidently, and Kate had to work not to snort at the irony of his choice of words. "Your cabin's in a prime location, and you'll have a lot of folks wanting to help you sell it. I wanted to meet you before you left, share some information about our company and hopefully move to the front of the line."

"Well, I'm sorry, but you've wasted a trip. I'm not selling."

He took a small step back, and his shoulders dropped a little. "You're not?"

"No."

"I'm sorry. Georgia didn't mention—"

"It's not her fault. I only told her yesterday," Kate offered.

"Oh." His smile slid off his face, but he held his card out to her, and she took it. "Well, if you ever decide to sell, I hope you'll consider using us."

"Thanks. I'll let you know if I do."

He turned and was nearly down the steps when a connection sparked in Kate's gut. "Mr. Norton?"

He stopped and swiveled, a renewed, slightly hopeful smile on his face.

"Have you been to my cabin recently? Anytime within the last month?"

His expression shifted, his eyebrows narrowing and back straightening ever-so-slightly. "I've driven by before, of course."

"You didn't take a stroll around the property just to see what was here? To check its condition and whatnot in preparation for listing it?"

"Well," he fumbled, his gloved hands clasping one another, "I did take a quick look around a couple of weeks ago. After Georgia mentioned it. Just to get the lay of the land. There didn't seem to be anyone staying here, so I didn't think it would be a problem. I'm sorry if I—"

"Did you see anyone? In the cabin or around it?" Her

words came hurriedly, tentative anticipation brewing within her.

"Well...no. There weren't any cars, and no one answered the door. I did knock, but—"

"What about the attic? Did you see anyone in the attic?" Kate pressed, now stepping fully through the doorway. Norton took a step backward in response.

"The attic? Ms. Palmer, I didn't go inside the house—"

"No, I'm sure you didn't. But did you see anyone in the attic window, maybe? When you walked around back."

He appraised her for a moment, and she knew he was trying to decide how much to say and whether he would find himself in hot water for being in the backyard without permission.

"I don't care if you went back there," she said, "I just need to know if you noticed anyone. In the attic window or anywhere else. Anyone or anything out of place."

"No, I...I didn't." He shrugged. "I did walk around the entire cabin, but I didn't see anyone in the, uh, attic window, or anywhere else. And as far as anything out of place, I wouldn't know if something was out of place or not. I haven't been here before."

"And there wasn't anything indicating someone was here? No tracks in the snow, or, I don't know, shoes by the door—"

"No," he interrupted. "Not that I noticed." A curious expression washed over his face, and he cleared his throat. "Have you been having problems with...unwanted visitors?"

Now she was the one carefully gauging her response. A home or neighborhood prone to break-ins would take a hit on valuation. She wasn't planning on selling, but if that changed at some point, she didn't need to be volunteering everything that had gone on recently. "Everything's fine. Just curious. Thank you for the information." She held up his business card. "I'll let you know if I change my mind about selling."

Without giving him a chance to ask more questions, she stepped inside and closed the door behind her. She leaned against it and exhaled. Ignoring the paper from the attic burning a hole in her pocket, she pulled out her phone.

18

"Did you send a real estate agent over here?" Kate asked as soon as Georgia answered the call. She sat on her fireplace hearth, the flames warming her back as she waited for Georgia to respond.

"What?" Georgia asked. "I don't—oh, wait. Carl? Did he get in touch with you?"

"He showed up here fifteen minutes ago, wanting me to hire him to sell the place."

"The day after Christmas?" Georgia asked, and Kate could hear the surprise in her friend's voice. "What was he thinking? I'm so sorry."

"Why didn't you tell me that you talked to him when I said I decided not to sell?"

"Kate, I forgot all about it. It was weeks ago when I ran into him. I thought I was helping. He's a good guy, and it's a reputable agency. I thought it might save you the trouble of finding someone."

"It's okay. It just surprised me, that's all. With everything that's gone on—I just wanted to make sure he was telling the truth about how he found out." She sighed. "It's fine, really. I'm just overwhelmed. The sheriff's deputies were here again this morning, and the evidence technician—"

"What did they find?" Georgia interrupted, her curiosity nearly palpable.

Kate first brought Georgia up to speed on the bizarre events of the night before and the disappearance of everything from the attic. After that, she filled her in on the investigation. "...But, essentially, *they* didn't find anything helpful. Hardly any prints, and not many they think they'll be able to use. And whoever cleaned out the attic took all their stuff. There are tracks in the snow leading from the porch and the back of the house, but they disappear in the woods. The deputies aren't very optimistic about catching whoever's responsible, for any or all of it."

"So...what happens next?" Georgia asked.

"It'll take days to get the fingerprint results back. If there is a match for Bleeker..." Kate's voice trailed off. "I suppose we'll cross that bridge when we come to it." She exhaled loudly. "But that isn't all."

"What do you mean?"

"The deputies didn't find anything, but I did," Kate said.

"What?"

"You guys are still coming for dinner, right?"

"Absolutely," Georgia replied.

"Well, come early. I want to show you this in person. I need to make sure I'm not going crazy."

Ten minutes later, Georgia sat on Kate's couch, while Rex perched in a side chair reading near the fire. Kate stood in front of Georgia, her heart thrumming. She held out the piece of paper from the attic.

"I found this in an open space between two floor joists, partially hidden by insulation. So we all missed it on the first look-through."

Georgia's green eyes traced the paper then cut back to Kate. "It's a receipt."

"Yeah, exactly," Kate said, tapping her toe nervously. "A receipt from the Fork & Spoon Bistro in Nashville. Erik and I used to go there all the time."

"And?"

"Don't you get it? Look at the date."

Georgia's eyes flitted down. When she glanced back up, her lids had narrowed. "Nooo…"

"Exactly. December 20th of last year. Three days before Erik left me. I actually *remember* that lunch," Kate replied.

"You remember a lunch from over a year ago?" Georgia echoed skeptically.

"When your husband leaves you out of the blue, you rethink everything that happened the month before. Yeah, I remember that lunch. And, before you ask, we used our credit card," she added, pointing to the last four digits of the card shown on the receipt. "So I know it's ours."

"Surely you're not thinking—"

"Georgia, how did that," Kate pointed an accusatory finger at the paper, "get up there?" she said, raising her finger toward the ceiling.

"Before you go running off with wild theories, couldn't

you have dropped it since you've been here? Was it your credit card or his?"

"We both had one on that account, and I don't remember who actually paid, but there's no way I came here with that receipt in one of my pockets. It would've been lost in the wash ages ago," Kate said. In her peripheral vision, she saw Rex twist in his seat and squint even harder at his book. He didn't like trouble, and from his shrunken shoulders and bowed head, she knew the conversation must be bothering him.

Maybe I should have talked with Georgia out of his earshot.

Then again, Rex also hated being singled out. He would know they were hiding something from him. Or he would assume they were talking about him, which would be even worse.

"It *probably* would have been destroyed in the wash, but you can't be one hundred percent certain. Sometimes things survive," Georgia argued.

"Yeah, sometimes. But not usually thin paper like this."

"Still, it's not impossible," Georgia said. "You've been up there working all over the place—pulling the tree down, moving boxes around. It could've fallen out of your pocket without you noticing."

"You're right, it's not impossible, but I just don't buy it," Kate replied.

"So, what, you're saying Erik left it up there? At some point between leaving you last year and today, *he* was in your attic?"

"I don't know how to explain it. That's what's nuts."

"Is it possible he came back for something? Something he stored up there?" Georgia asked.

"He didn't keep anything at the cabin. And I think the last

time we were here was...well, in the spring, right? We had that barbecue with you guys—long before that lunch."

"In the spring," Rex muttered darkly. "The spring before he left you."

Kate's gut tightened, hearing how bitter he sounded. Rex had always been protective of her, even as a kid, and clearly he was harboring angry feelings over what Erik had done.

"No," Kate said, wanting to shift the focus back to the receipt, "I don't think Erik came here for something and dropped this. And I also don't think he was the one camping out up there."

"I'm lost. Exactly what *are* you saying?" Georgia asked, her face contorted in confusion.

"Okay...now just give this a minute, but...what about Bleeker?"

"What about him?"

"What if *he* had the receipt and dropped it when he was camping out upstairs. What if he had something to do with Erik?"

"Had something to do with him, how?" Georgia asked.

"I know we didn't talk a ton of specifics about Bleeker when it was going on, but I did tell you how threatening he was at the end, didn't I?" Kate replied.

"Yeah," Georgia answered, her stare urging Kate to get to the point.

"It wasn't me he was threatening, really. It was Erik. The whole 'you-belong-to-me-not-him' thing."

"Okay," Georgia said.

Kate's insides flipped at having to spell it out. She would have felt less ridiculous about suggesting it if Georgia had come to the same conclusion. She inhaled a deep breath through her nose, then exhaled. "What if Bleeker acted on his threats? What if he took Erik, kidnapped him or...worse? What if that's how he got the receipt and hung on to it for some weird reason and then came up here to be close to me and dropped it—"

"Wait," Georgia said, sitting up straight and pressing her palms toward Kate. "Erik has not been kidnapped."

"How do we know?" Kate said, slinging her arms wide. "And maybe he didn't kidnap him. Maybe he," she paused, her heart catching in her throat at the notion, "killed him."

Georgia's eyes widened, and Rex dove so far into his book it was practically touching his face.

"Kate, come on," Georgia implored, her eyes brimming with pity. "Don't do this to yourself. Martin Bleeker did not kidnap Erik, and he certainly didn't kill him. You're taking this one little piece of paper and constructing an outlandish story to explain it—"

"Have you got a better story? Because someone's been in this house. Someone's stolen things. Someone was *living* in the attic, and last night somebody was banging on my door like something out of a horror movie. Someone, maybe even two someones, left tracks coming and going from the cabin—front and back, mind you—and someone," she pointed to the receipt Georgia held, shaking her finger, "dropped that. And if it wasn't me, and it wasn't Erik...you tell me who else besides Martin Bleeker makes sense."

19

What are they doing in there?

Once again, the thick web of woods camouflaged him well. It was dusk and getting darker by the minute. Soon he would be nearly invisible even if they were looking straight at him.

He watched the windows of her cabin, where she and her friends were cozied-up inside. She had drawn the drapes across the windows, so all he could see were shadows moving and a faint flickering from what he presumed was the fire.

She was learning. She knew he was out there. Or suspected. She had grown much less trusting since arriving that first night, when she left the drapes open to watch the snow.

And for good reason.

Not that it would make any difference.

20

Once they moved off the topic of the receipt and what might actually be going on—Kate planned to hash it out more with Georgia without Rex around—Rex slowly came to life. He helped with the final touches on the dinner of chili, slaw, and cornbread Kate had made, and when she asked what game they should play, he enthusiastically picked Monopoly™, another of his and Pop's favorites. That led to an hour and a half of buying and selling and an unusually bold Rex declaring himself "King of the World" when Kate went bankrupt.

"We watched *Titanic* last month," Georgia whispered in explanation.

After that, Rex went back to his book while Georgia pulled out her laptop. "I brought this to show you," she said, opening a list she had made of real estate management companies that could handle the upkeep of the cabin and its rental to tourists.

"This woman I actually know," Georgia said, pointing to

the face of a middle-aged woman with a brown bob and narrow-framed glasses, "and she's really trustworthy. Now this one," she said, clicking over to a different screen where another agency's website was waiting, "I don't know personally, but I've heard good things from some people in town that used them."

They stayed until just before nine, going over rental possibilities and squeezing in one more card game at Rex's insistence. Finally, Georgia begged off, saying she was exhausted and that they both had to work the next day. Christmas had fallen on a Sunday, and both of them had only been given Monday off—Rex from his construction job and Georgia from her part-time position with a time-share company in Maryville. According to Georgia, the job filled the financial gap between their expenses and their income from Rex's paycheck and sales of her artwork. "It also helps me not go stir-crazy, seeing other faces a few times a week," she admitted to Kate.

Now Kate stood over the sink, using a scouring pad to scrub the pot she had cooked the chili in, the aroma of garlic, tomatoes, and chili powder still lingering in the air. Georgia and Rex had helped clean up, so fortunately this was all that was left to do, because she was feeling pretty beat too. Her plan was to go to bed as soon as possible, then get up early and spend the day online and on the phone. She needed to find a new place to live in Nashville and start reaching out to those local real estate management companies Georgia had come up with.

Then her phone rang and changed everything.

Kate stepped into the foyer of Georgia's cabin and her mouth dropped. The place looked like a tornado hit it. Drawers were dumped out, cabinets opened, and wires were strewn across the entertainment system, the equipment they had belonged to, gone. Georgia and Deputy Lyle stood by the couch, talking. Another deputy, not Deputy Cawthorne, walked through the room, taking photos.

Georgia spotted Kate and mouthed, *give me a minute,* before continuing her discussion. She pointed toward the kitchen, though, and Kate followed her finger to Rex, standing in a corner out of the way.

"I can't believe it!" Kate exclaimed, walking over and hugging him. "I'm so sorry," she said as she pulled back to get a good look at him. "Are you okay?"

His face was a portrait of defeat. "I don't like that someone did this."

"No, I bet you don't. I wouldn't either. I *didn't*. You already know something similar happened at my cabin."

Rex nodded. "It's happening a lot. Georgia says it looks like some bad elements have discovered the Ridge." He turned away to face the room but stayed close, sidling up to her so their shoulders were touching. "I'm really sorry. I know it's not what you expected when you decided to keep Pop's cabin."

"No, it's not." Bloodroot Ridge had always been a safe place. Practically no crime to speak of. Now it seemed to be everywhere she turned.

Georgia walked over and Kate hugged her hard. "What happened?"

"No idea. We got home from your place and found it like this."

"This is a lot more than eyeglasses and a perfume bottle," Kate commented, wondering how she would have felt if she had found her cabin in this state when she arrived. Of course, Georgia's stuff was much newer and nicer. Much more tempting for a burglar.

Deputy Lyle caught Kate's eye and nodded in acknowledgement before returning to his examination of the ransacked built-in shelves.

"This isn't even his shift," Georgia told Kate, tilting her head at Deputy Lyle. "They called him in because he's been handling your case. I guess they think there could be a connection."

"That's not good."

"No, it's not." Georgia frowned. "I heard them whispering about 'a string' of robberies, probably thinking about you and Donovan's Mercantile, and who knows what else. If this turns into a pattern and word gets out, it'll really hurt the area's value. Another reason it's good you're not selling right now, I guess. I feel bad for other people, though. I know there's a couple of places for sale up the road."

"Any idea how they got in?" Kate asked.

"The front door was jimmied. Wouldn't have been difficult. We don't even use the deadbolt most of the time," Georgia said.

"Does the rest of the house look like this?"

"Pretty much. My office is a disaster. They found some cash I was hiding in there." She sighed heavily. "It could've been worse. They didn't get my computer since I took it with me tonight. That would've been a nightmare. Unfortunately, Rex's iPad was in the rec room, and they got that. He's...not happy."

Rex didn't deal with normal change well. A violation like this and losing something as personal as his iPad would have tough emotional consequences. Kate's blood boiled at the thought of what he must be going through. Maybe getting him out of there for the night would help him process it.

"Do you guys want to stay with me?" she asked.

"No, we'll be fine. I don't think they'll be here long," Georgia said, nodding at the deputies. "Deputy Lyle said they don't expect to find much. They think these guys were professionals. Probably watched for us to leave, then came in while we were at your place."

"Do they think the burglars might have been the same people involved with my cabin?"

"He didn't say."

"What about tracks or footprints?"

Georgia shrugged. "There are some out there, but they're mixed with ours. They don't think they'll help."

"So basically the same situation as my cabin."

"Basically."

Kate noticed Deputy Lyle dusting for fingerprints along the entertainment center where the flat screen television was missing. "They're not sending out their evidence tech to do that?"

"He said the tech's not available, and we wanted to get this over with. I don't want to leave the house a mess until he can get here. It's not," she cut her eyes momentarily to Rex, "healthy. He says they're all trained to lift prints, if needed. I can't imagine they'll find anything other than ours anyway. These guys seemed to know what they're doing. Probably wore gloves."

"I'm really sorry, Georgia."

"They didn't get anything that can't be replaced. I keep my nice jewelry and the guns locked in the gun safe. Our insurance deductible's pretty high, though, so I guess we'll get stuck shelling out for replacements for the TV, stereo, Rex's iPad." She winced. "Wow, that's gonna add up. Not to mention the grand of cash they stole from my office." Georgia's face darkened. "I just don't get it. We've never had problems like this before. I hate what the area's turning into."

"Maybe it'll be a one-off. Or I guess, a two-off, if you count my place."

"You're forgetting about Donovan's."

Kate's heart sank. "Right." She sighed. It really did seem like the area had become a magnet for trouble. "Well, if you won't stay at my place tonight, can I at least come over tomorrow and help clean up?"

Georgia slung an arm around Kate, resting her head on Kate's shoulder. "That would be great. We should be home around five thirty. I'll bring pizza."

"We can crank up the music and turn it into a dance party, right, Rex?" Kate suggested, tugging on his sleeve. For a quiet guy, oddly enough the one loud thing he really enjoyed was a dance party. But only a very *specific* kind of dance party.

"80s playlist?" he said, his face turning up slightly.

"What else?" Kate answered, earning a squeeze on the arm and a warm smile from Georgia in return.

21

Kate lay in bed, staring at the ceiling, processing, trying to understand.

So much had gone wrong in the last twelve months, and the last three days had just been more of the same. She had come to the cabin ready to sell it even though she didn't want to, because at least that would have finally brought an end to the divorce. But once she arrived, it hadn't felt right to let the cabin go. Deciding to keep it had made her feel better than she had felt in a year. It was supposed to be a new beginning.

So why was it still just one problem after another?

It wasn't as if she had made the decision lightly. She had prayed over it after the idea occurred to her on Christmas Eve. She had lain right there in that bed, quietly, listening with her heart, until peace *and* certainty had come. And in that moment she had been sure. The next morning—Christmas morning—she was still sure. But now, with everything that was happening, she was starting to doubt.

Had she been right to change her plan?

What if she couldn't make it work?

What if she couldn't find an affordable place close enough to her office?

What if, after trying, I end up having to sell the cabin anyway? And what if, by then, it's worth less than it is now? What do I do then?

Trust.

The word echoed in her mind, as it had so many times over the last year.

Trust.

Trust that God has a plan. Trust that the hard things have a purpose. She had been holding onto that, holding onto her faith despite everything. Because she knew that God uses even the awful stuff. That He doesn't waste our pain.

She sighed and rolled over. Her faith, her God, that was what—was *who*—had held her together. She knew that. She believed that. But this craziness was pushing her to the brink of what she could bear.

How much longer would she have to wait before she had some normalcy again?

Surely it couldn't be much longer. Surely the worst was over.

It wasn't.

At eight a.m., Kate sat on the tile floor of her master bathroom, her legs drawn to her chest, knees under her chin as she stared at the mirror, the blood in her veins colder than the snow on the ground outside.

Scrawled in uneven capital letters on the glass, in one of her reddish lipsticks, were the words:

I'M NOT GONE

She had come in to wash her face and seen them, sending paralytic fear coursing through her body. She screamed, dropping to the floor as her legs gave out. She hadn't moved since and had no idea how long she had been there, as her phone sat useless on her nightstand.

I'm not gone.

Her mind raced in loops. *Who is "I"? Bleeker? Someone else? What do they want from me?*

She sucked in a quivering breath.

Whoever it was walked right through my bedroom to get to the bathroom. While I slept. Again.

A shiver ripped through her.

Did they come close to my bed? Did they watch me sleep?

The terrifying thoughts fought for space in her head along with all of the "how" questions.

How did they get in?

How did I not hear them?

Someone had opened a door or window, come inside, gone into her bathroom, opened a drawer, dug out her lipstick, written a message and left, all without her hearing *any* of it.

I'm not gone.

Another shiver shook her. *What if they literally aren't gone? What if they're still in the cabin right now?*

Her rubbery legs worked to support her as she sprang up and ran to her bed. She dropped to her knees, lowering her head to look beneath it, already shoving an arm under the frame to retrieve the rifle.

It wasn't there.

Shoving herself against the nightstand and gasping for air that wasn't coming, she snatched her phone up and dialed 9-1-1.

Kate sat on a barstool, her shoe tapping nervously on the footrest, Deputy Lyle standing beside her.

"I think it's time for you to seriously consider leaving the cabin, Ms. Palmer," he said, his brow furrowed, feet shoulder-width apart in an authoritative stance. "There's clearly more going on here than meets the eye, and until we know what it is, you're not safe."

"You think I don't know that!" she shot back, louder than she meant to. Her fingertips were tingling as she downed another gulp of herbal tea, but the brew and warmth were doing nothing to calm her. "This has got to be Bleeker. Nothing else makes sense. No vagrant would keep coming back like this."

"No, you're right," he agreed. "It's unlikely. But we can't just jump to conclusions. Is there anyone other than Bleeker who would have a reason to..." His words trailed off as he seemed to be searching for the right one, "...stalk you like this?"

"No."

"What about your ex-husband?"

"My ex-husband is off with his new wife in South Carolina. I haven't seen him in a year, and he's got no reason to harass me. I've given him everything he wants." She sighed, tossing her head to one shoulder as she reconsidered. "Well..."

"Well, what?" Deputy Lyle asked.

"The whole reason I came up here was to prep the cabin for sale. I need the cash to wrap up the property division from the divorce. But after getting here, I decided to keep it. I'm going to sell the Nashville property instead—anyway, it doesn't matter because he's still getting his money. Believe me, I'm not even on his radar." She swallowed, knowing it was time to fill the deputy in on the receipt. "If Erik's involved, it's only because of Bleeker." She retrieved the piece of paper from her purse and handed it to him, explaining how she found it in the attic and what that had to mean.

"You're suggesting Bleeker did something to your husband in order to get this?"

"I'm suggesting that either Erik had to be up there or Bleeker, who somehow got the receipt from Erik. But I can't think of a single reason Erik would be in the attic. So my bet is on Bleeker."

"And you think he, what, stole this off your ex-husband?"

"Well, that would be the best-case scenario. That he stalked him, or got it from his trash or something. Worst case scenario is that he did something to my ex-husband and got it then."

"What do you mean by '*did*' something to your husband?"

"Bleeker threatened him in the past. What if he followed through?"

"But you've had communications with your ex-husband, right?"

"I've spoken with him on the phone a couple of times.

There were a few emails before the lawyers took over. He remarried pretty fast. I haven't really wanted to speak with him."

"But in all those communications he didn't say anything about a run-in with Bleeker? He's been fine all that time, right? Living his life?"

She nodded.

"What about social media? I'm assuming he's on it?"

Again, she nodded. Of course she wanted the explanation to be something other than Bleeker harming Erik. Even after everything, she didn't want that. "I know it's a wild theory, and I'm not saying it's the only option but—"

"If Bleeker did drop that receipt, it's more likely he got it by breaking into your Nashville place, isn't it? Maybe he went through your ex-husband's things or just came across it. You said he broke in once before?" Deputy Lyle asked.

"Yeah," she answered, and as she listened to his theory, she realized her pulse was slowing to something that felt less like a heart attack. His idea made sense, and was definitely more plausible than hers.

"He would know that was a restaurant you and your husband frequented. So maybe he kept the receipt as some weird trophy. I'm not saying that's exactly what happened. I'm just saying that there are other explanations for how it got in your attic besides your husband being kidnapped by your stalker."

"I agree. I just said it was one possibility for how Bleeker got that receipt and that him being up there makes a lot more sense than Erik rummaging around my attic." She cocked her head. "Have you gotten any fingerprint results? And what did the Nashville police say about Bleeker? Did they talk to him?"

"No results yet. I promise I'll update you when and if we get a match." He sniffed and shifted his stance. "As for speaking with Bleeker, Metro Nashville says they can't find him."

Kate's mouth dropped, and heat flashed through her. "They don't know where he is?"

"He maintains a residence in the city, but he isn't there now and from the looks of it, he hasn't been for a while."

She splayed her hands. "Are they going to look for him? Put out an APB or whatever?"

"No. They don't have cause to look for him."

She guffawed, throwing a hand toward her bedroom. "Well, I've got a mirror that says differently."

"That doesn't prove who your stalker is. Just that you've got one," Deputy Lyle argued.

"You can't be serious."

"And you can't go making assumptions. It doesn't work that way. Right now, the best thing for you to do is to go back home. Whoever this is wasn't bothering you there, right?"

She stared at him.

"Right?" he repeated.

She folded her arms. "No."

"Then go back home where you're safe. Where there are more people around and you're not in the woods alone."

"I'm not alone. I have friends here."

"Ms. Palmer, they can't help with this. What if, next time, you wake up and find him—whoever it is—standing over your bed? You don't have your rifle anymore, do you?"

It was a harsh reminder that whoever was doing this had also stolen her only means of protecting herself. Kate covered her face with her hands, then ran them over her long blond hair, twisting the ends before letting go. "If I go, who's to say he won't follow me?"

"I can't promise he won't. But it's safer than being here. And while I can't assume this is Bleeker's doing, I will admit that it seems the most likely explanation. You go home and I'll ask Metro Nashville to do some drive-by checks on your house for a couple of weeks. You might even consider hiring someone for protection—"

"I can't afford—"

"Only for a little while," he finished. "Or have a friend or family member stay. Having another person around will likely scare the guy off."

"And what about the cabin?"

"We'll continue investigating, and we'll keep an eye on the place. If someone starts using it, we'll catch 'em. But for now, cut your holiday short, head home, and get some protection in place," Deputy Lyle said, his voice stern.

When Kate finally locked the door behind them, something had changed. She dropped onto the couch, taking a long look around the room, listening to the fire crackle in the quiet. This was her cabin. Her safe place.

Hers.

At least, it had been. But now even that had been taken from her. Because Deputy Lyle was right.

The only way she would be safe was to go home.

22

At three thirty Kate stood at the front door to Georgia and Rex's cabin. The plan had been to meet them when they got home from work in a couple of hours, but that was before some crazy person had gone psycho on her mirror.

She was leaving, and she needed to tell them in person. She had already packed her bags and driven over with them in the car. When Georgia and Rex got home, she would explain, have a quick dinner, then get on the road.

But she wanted to do one last thing first.

Kate called Rex right after the deputies left around eight, catching him as he was leaving for his shift. She explained how she wanted to surprise Georgia by cleaning up everything in their cabin before they got home and asked Rex to drop their house key off with her on his way to work.

Now Kate held Rex's full key ring—she had chuckled when he handed over the whole thing instead of simply removing the one key—and used the one labeled "house" to enter through the front door.

She found the place was still the ransacked mess from the night before.

They must have gone straight to bed without touching a thing.

Kate started in the kitchen, closing drawers, putting contents back in cabinets, and straightening stacks of paper on the counter. From there she began working on the living room—bundling cords with rubber bands she had found in a drawer, straightening shelves and cushions, and returning books to their rightful places from where they had been tossed on the floor, in what Kate could only guess was a search for hidden valuables.

Shattered glass from several framed photographs, carelessly cast aside, peppered the hardwood floor. Kate retrieved a broom from the closet and swept up as much as she could, then used the vacuum. She dusted, swept, straightened and vacuumed over and over until finally the room looked like itself again, albeit missing a few items.

It actually didn't take as long as she expected. The mess had looked a lot worse than it was. Still, she relished the thought of Georgia coming home and finding the place put back together. She knew Georgia would be happy, even though she would probably fuss at her for doing it.

A twinge of sadness pricked her heart. If she was honest with herself, chances were she was going to be selling the cabin after all. She doubted she would ever feel safe there, and she couldn't go much longer without a cash influx if she was going to pay Erik off by the settlement deadline.

If she sold, it wasn't likely she would see much of Georgia and Rex anymore. Not unless she made a special trip out there. As much as she wanted to believe she would make the effort, life usually interfered with those kinds of things, despite a person's best intentions. She could—she would—invite them to visit her in Nashville, but the same would be true for them. When people lose the things they have in common, they often just go their separate ways.

Kate shook her head. Losing yet another person—persons—from her life seemed so unfair.

But, lately, unfair was all she seemed to get.

23

She's inside right now.

He could feel the moment coming upon him like a train hurtling toward a station, the inevitable confrontation rushing closer and closer with every passing second.

Why did she have to go in there? Why didn't she just leave?

If she wasn't going to leave, he would have to act. This hadn't been a problem before—when it was just a possibility. But now that it was finally time, he found himself reevaluating the risks.

And the costs. If it actually came down to carrying it out... could he do it? Did he really want to add that to his list of regrets?

That list was pretty long already.

24

Kate worked her way farther into the house. The spare rooms weren't too bad. Mostly just empty drawers pulled out and turned over. When she got to their personal bedrooms, she left those alone, feeling that would be too much of an invasion of privacy. Georgia's office was worse than the family room, plus it was covered in papers dumped from wherever they had been stored. Since Kate had no idea how it had been organized, she couldn't do much beyond making piles and vacuuming, so she decided to leave it until last, if she had time, and headed upstairs.

Up in the rec room, all the cushions from the U-shaped couch lay haphazardly discarded on the floor. As she tucked them back into place, Kate wondered what the burglars could possibly have been looking for underneath them. Her eyes flicked to the drawers of the entertainment center and the DVDs scattered on the floor, and she pictured the downstairs, with all the open drawers and the same "searched" quality about it. If she didn't know better, she would have said the whole thing looked more like an attempt to find something, rather than a run-of-the-mill robbery. But things had been stolen, including Rex's iPad from this very room. It was just Georgia and Rex's luck that they had been hit by overly thorough burglars.

By four forty she had finished all the rooms except the office. She hustled downstairs, hoping to at least put it in a better state, leaving Georgia and Rex only their own bedrooms to deal with.

A good going-away present.

As she stepped through the office doorway, her phone blasted the theme song from her favorite detective show, the jarring tones causing her heart to leap into her throat even though she had heard them a million times.

I've got to change that. I have enough things making me jumpy already.

She glanced at the caller ID, which read "Donner County Sheriff's Department," and felt another jolt to her nervous system.

"Hello?" she answered.

"Ms. Palmer, this is Deputy Lyle."

Her chest tightened. "Did you hear something?"

"We just got the fingerprint results. None were a match for Martin Bleeker or anyone else in our system."

"But that doesn't mean it wasn't Bleeker. It just means he didn't leave prints or wiped them off," she argued.

"No. Metro Nashville Police found Bleeker. He actually doesn't reside in Nashville anymore. He owns the property there but rents it out. He lives in Portland, Oregon, now. Runs a manufacturing plant, and he's been there every day for the last two weeks, except for the last few when he flew out to be with family in Texas for Christmas. Apparently, there's plenty of witnesses to back him up. So there's no way he's been here, harassing you."

Kate felt as if she had dropped through the floor and was still going. It wasn't that she wanted it to be Bleeker, but at least he was a known entity. If it wasn't Bleeker, then where did that leave her? And what about the receipt? "So now what?"

"Now that we know what we know about the prints and Bleeker, I'm going to reach out to your ex-husband at the number you gave me."

"I don't even know if that's still his number. Like I said, I haven't spoken to him in months."

"I'll get in touch with him one way or another. Assuming he's still alive and kicking, which seems likely given what you've told me, and has an alibi for the last week, we won't have any other rabbits to chase after that. We'll be keeping an eye on the place. But I still strongly suggest you head home for safety's sake."

"I'm going home today," she answered, hearing the note of bitterness in her tone, but not caring. "So if there's any activity at the cabin, it won't be me."

"Good decision. You let us know if anything changes on your end."

She hung up, disappointment, confusion, and fear squeezing her like a tightly wrapped shroud. None of it made sense.

Plus, if they didn't have answers now, she probably wasn't going to be able to hold onto the cabin long enough to get them.

"Office" was only a half-accurate description of the room. It was actually a hybrid of an art studio and office. One side housed a desk, and behind that, a filing cabinet and bookshelves resting on a credenza. File folders and papers were scattered over everything in that area. The other side of the room held several easels displaying works-in-progress in bright hues of oil paint. Georgia had always been partial to vivid colors, most of her paintings were of the contemporary impressionism variety—bold and dreamy takes on the natural world.

Erik would love these, Kate thought before she could stop herself. She wished Georgia had shown them to her when she came over on Christmas. Kate had asked Georgia about her current work, but Georgia had brushed her off, saying she was in a bit of a rut. But these didn't look like a rut. These looked inspired.

Kate ran a hand over one of the dry paintings, a depiction of a Smoky Mountain hillside bathed in mountain laurel. Another portrayed a woody grove covered in bloodroot flowers with their stark white petals and yellow stamens. There were others, all in varying stages of completion, full of nature and an otherworldly quality. Pride blossomed in Kate. These were really good. Some of her favorites featured an indistinct figure in the distant background, seeming to stare wistfully off into whatever lay beyond, in the depths of the painting.

Maybe I can sell these to clients, Kate thought. *It would be a win-win. I would be getting her name out in the city, she would have a reason to visit, and for Georgia, the money would be really good...*

"Okay, enough, you're running out of time," Kate said, pulling herself away from the mesmerizing artwork to begin culling through the papers. A few frames had been broken in here too, and she carefully gathered and disposed of the glass as she stacked and sorted. She tried her best not to look too closely at the papers, as they were none of her business. But making piles at least made the room seem less of a disaster. As she considered trying to protect Georgia's privacy, Kate bit her lip. She would have wagered Georgia wouldn't mind her being in here, but now, seeing the paintings she had intentionally kept from her...

Maybe this was a bad decision.

The problem was she had already started. It seemed *more* wrong to undo the picking up she had finished to try to hide the fact that she had been in the room.

Oh well. In for a penny...she'll forgive me.

She continued collecting the papers, now turning the pages over so Georgia would know she hadn't looked at any of them. There were labeled files too, but fortunately, most of them weren't open, so she didn't even see what—

Kate's breath hitched in her throat. The manila file she just picked up had a number and identifying marker stamped on the front lower right corner. One she recognized.

This file is from the offices of:
Dr. Erik Palmer, MD
Palmer Psychiatry, Inc.
Nashville, Tennessee
File No. 00001768

25

The file burned in her hands.

This thing, here in this room, was utterly wrong.

I shouldn't look.

I should put it down.

But the wheels in her mind were spinning, cogs and treads clicking into place at frightening speed.

There has to be a benign explanation for the file being here. I can just ask Georgia about it when she gets home.

Or not.

Whispering an "I'm sorry" unheard by anyone, Kate flipped open the file on the desk.

There were perfectly acceptable reasons why Georgia might have decided not to tell her that Rex had been seeing Erik for therapy. Confidentiality for one.

Or the fact that Georgia might have thought it would hurt Kate to bring up Erik.

Or that it would have angered Kate to know that, in leaving, Erik had also hurt Rex by costing him a trusted counselor.

Or simply because it really wasn't any of Kate's business.

But when she opened it, she realized it wasn't any of those reasons.

Because it wasn't Rex's file.

It was Georgia's.

A low buzzing sounded in Kate's ears as she stared at the page attached to the inside left flap that listed Georgia's basic information. Her eyes drifted to the right flap, where the records of Georgia's sessions were affixed with a two-hole punch fastener.

I could shut it right now.

Before I see anything.

It's not too late—but then it was, because of the one sentence that caught her eye.

Patient has developed a romantic fixation on the therapist.

Then the world opened up and swallowed Kate Palmer.

She woke on the office floor, Georgia's file inches from her hands. She was hot and cold at the same time, oddly rejuvenated and drained of all energy.

She wasn't one to pass out. Not even when she found Erik's letter. But this was more than that. This was truth and lies and a loudspeaker screaming, *Danger, Danger!*

She pushed up into a sitting position and grabbed the file again.

How long was I out?

She checked her phone. Not long at all, it seemed. That was good. But it was also after 5:00. And that wasn't. Georgia and Rex could walk in at any minute.

She tore into the file again.

The more she read, the sicker she felt, until she had to press a hand to her forehead, wiping away the clammy sweat gathered there. Confusion and panic roiled within her until she caught herself nearly hyperventilating. After working to slow her breath, she kept reading.

Georgia had begun seeing Erik a full year before he left. She initially came for help with the stress of serving as Rex's guardian. Once a month, she had driven to Nashville for sessions. But the topic quickly turned from Rex to Georgia's insecurities and self-worth issues, unhealthy attachments to men she had dated and broken-up with, then finally, to her attachment to Erik.

Notes recorded small red flags—hugs that lasted too long, kisses on the cheek, and frequent calls outside of session times. Showing up at the office without an appointment. Showing up at their house.

She was at our house?

Kate's mind whirled, trying to reconcile her reality with what she was reading. When had Georgia come? And how could Erik have not told her?

But of course he wouldn't have told her. Patient confidentiality overrode almost everything.

Georgia's behavior escalated until finally peaking when she declared her love for Erik during a session in October. He noted that he advised her that he wouldn't be able to continue as her therapist and referred her to someone else. She hadn't taken it well, ripping up the new therapist's business card and storming out, promising that Erik would be sorry.

Two months later, Erik was gone.

I'm not gone.

The scrawled red words from her mirror crashed into Kate's brain like an eighteen-wheeler through a plate glass window. Only this one both shattered her, then, like footage rewound, put the pieces back together. She spun around, spotted what she was looking for on Georgia's desk and flew to it.

This was a bottomless pit, and Kate was forever falling, one dark, destructive realization after the other pulling her deeper and deeper toward a horrible truth.

She reached for Georgia's laptop, sitting open and unlocked on her desk. It occurred to her that this was odd, but Kate shoved the thought aside, her eyes hungrily searching the computer's desktop. Off to the right was a file marked "The Good Doctor." Kate clicked on it, and its contents spilled out.

Dozens of photos of the woman Kate knew as Miranda Palmer, Erik's new wife, covered the screen. Only they weren't actually of "Miranda Palmer." They were stock photos, clearly identified as such by the file names which included the name of the site they had come from.

Miranda Palmer didn't exist.

There were also stock photos of locations—the very shots

posted on Miranda's and Erik's Instagram accounts. Then there were the compilations. Photos Georgia must have created in an application, merging photos of people with locations to create fiction. To make it look like those people had been to those places. Some of them even had "Miranda" and Erik in the same photo.

This wasn't something everyone could do, but it wouldn't have been hard for Georgia. Though Georgia majored in fine art in college, Kate also knew she had minored in graphic design in the hopes of merging the two skill sets.

But where had Georgia pulled Erik's photos from? Grabbing old photos from Kate's own Facebook account seemed most likely. It had held plenty of them before Kate took them all down.

She could've easily modified them so I wouldn't recognize them as ones I'd seen before.

Now that she thought about it, most of the photos on Miranda's and Erik's Instagram accounts hadn't even had Erik in them. They were mostly of Miranda. But there were just enough of Erik to make it look like he was there. Which now, it seemed he hadn't been.

So if there was no Miranda Palmer...where was Erik?

Horror gripped Kate like a vise around her ribcage. If Erik hadn't left her a year ago, then what had actually happened to him?

He's dead! a panic-stricken voice shouted in her head. *She killed him!*

"No, no, no," she muttered out loud, as reason fought against despair.

Remember the message? I'M NOT GONE.

It wasn't Bleeker that left that message. He was in Texas.

She took several deep breaths, steadying herself against the desk. If Erik had left that message, then he was still alive. But then why was he still hiding from her, allowing the charade to continue? That didn't make sense.

Which made it more likely it was left by Georgia.

Or Rex.

"No! Not Rex," Kate barked, arguing with her own thoughts. There was no way she could believe Rex was involved in...this...whatever this was. He was too good a soul.

But why would Georgia leave me that message? What could she hope to gain by scaring me, making me think a stalker was terrorizing me, burglarizing my house, coming for me...

The avalanche of truth fell upon Kate, and for a dozen heartbeats she stared out the window, frozen in finally understanding, paralyzed by the realization that everything she had believed for a year was a lie.

But then her instincts kicked in, and she moved fiercely and with purpose, not having to wonder what to do next. Not even for a second. Because she had been coming there almost her entire life.

And she held the key to ending the whole thing.

26

Literally. Rex's keys jangled in her hand, the freezing air biting her, clawing at her exposed skin as she ran from the cabin to the shed on the other side of the driveway. She had grabbed the keys off the kitchen counter on the way out the front door and now fumbled with them, searching for the right one. Finally, she found the one labeled "shed" and turned it in the padlock on the shed door.

Kate threw open the door to the old wooden building. It slammed into the wall or whatever was piled behind it, but she didn't bother to look because her eyes were searching for only one thing.

The door in the floor that led to the in-ground tornado shelter.

Pushing past lawn equipment and random gardening supplies, she stopped at a wheelbarrow filled with concrete blocks parked squarely in the center of the room, right on top of the metal door. Heaving it by its wooden handles, Kate dragged the wheelbarrow out of the way then knelt down beside the door. A latch, locked by yet another padlock, had been added where previously there had only been a handle. She flipped through the keys, yipped when she actually found one labeled "lock" and used it. Tossing the lock aside, she lifted the door by its handle, opening it as far as she could and propping it against the wheelbarrow.

The same ladder they had used when playing there as children was still secured to the shelter's edge by hooks at the top, the rest descending into the depths below. She got down on the floor again and, lying flat on her belly, shone her phone flashlight into the six-by-nine hole in the ground.

Light fell across the face of Erik Palmer, and Kate gasped violently—not only from the shock of actually finding him there, but because of the state of him. He was thinner and paler than he had ever been. He lay on a cot positioned beside a small table that held the barely touched components of what must have been breakfast and several bottles of water.

"Kate?" His voice was scratchy, and he blinked hard, shaking his head, clearly confused by what he was seeing.

"Erik!" She clambered down the ladder so fast that she slipped on the last two rungs, landing hard. She dropped to her knees beside Erik's bed, embracing him and sobbing. "Erik! What...I can't believe—"

She rose up, letting her eyes rake over Erik's body. He was dressed in a dark sweatshirt that looked two sizes too big. A wool blanket draped the middle of his torso, his legs poking out at the bottom revealing sweatpants and thick socks. She fell on him again, hugging him tightly, her face buried in his chest. She felt one of his arms rise slowly, his hand feebly patting her back.

"Kate?" It came out as nothing more than a choked whisper, raspy and aged. She pulled back, brushing his cheek with her thumb as he blinked, confusion etched in the lines of his face. Lines that seemed so much deeper than they had a year ago. "Kate? Am I...dreaming? Is that you?"

"I'm here, I'm here," she said, clasping his cheeks with her hands and leaning in to kiss him.

"I thought...I don't believe it." Suddenly, his expression shifted, his eyes alight with fear and his body tensing. "You shouldn't be here! Kate, listen—"

"It's all right. I promise. No one else is home yet." She pulled out her phone to call 9-1-1, but found she had no reception ten feet underground. "Okay, we'll call up top. Come on," she said, sliding her arms beneath his and pulling him into a sitting position.

"We have to go fast," he urged. But even as he said it, his movements were sluggish, as if trapped underwater. "Before they realize." His words were slurred too.

They've been drugging him.

She pulled him to the ladder where she put him on it and pushed. His climb was slow and labored, and more than once she worried he would fall back on her. Even with the weight loss, he would do a lot of damage to her. She didn't want to think about what would happen if she broke a leg or something and they couldn't get away fast enough.

But he never faltered. First, Erik crawled out, then Kate as, kneeling, he reached a hand back to help her. She felt the familiar sensation of his fingers grasping hers, pulling weakly but clearly determined to get her out.

When they both finally stood, and she got a good look at him, the shadows cast in the dimly lit shed revealed him to be a shell of the man she had last seen a year ago. Even so, he grabbed her with a strength she wouldn't have thought possible and pulled her into his chest. Kate wrapped her arms around him and squeezed.

"I'm so sorry," he whispered, choking on tears. "I'm so sorry. I didn't leave you. I didn't—"

"I know," she said, leaning back to look into his eyes and feeling warm tears rolling down her own cheeks. "But we've got to go." She released him, pulling her phone out and dialing 9-1-1, then holding it to her ear. "Come on," she said, pulling him out the door into the open air, where snow had begun falling again.

"Kate!" he grunted, his eyes wide as he stared off into the snow behind her.

He was clearly confused, probably in some sort of drug-induced stupor. "Yes, it's me," she said, an electric current of nervous energy racing through her, knowing they had to move, and move fast. "Erik," she said, taking him by the shoulder, "my car's in the drive and—"

"Kate!"

The barking voice came from behind and pierced her like a spike through her heart. Kate whipped her head around to see Georgia standing in front of the cabin's side porch, holding a rifle in her hands.

"No, no, no..." Erik droned, his weak gaze tracking Georgia. He hadn't been confused at all. He had just seen Georgia before she did.

"You can't leave, Kate," Georgia called out. "And you can't take him. I won't let you."

Georgia was right about one thing. They couldn't leave. At

least not in Kate's car. They would have to cross in front of her to get to it.

"Don't be stupid," Georgia said. "You need to do exactly what I tell you."

Even from across the twenty-yard distance, Kate detected something alien about her friend. Maybe it was her rigid stance, or the way she tilted her head forward, creating curtains of dark hair on either side of her face, casting her features in sinister shadow. Or maybe it was the blackness in her gaze that sent chills down Kate's spine.

This was not her friend. That person was gone.

This person had made Erik disappear. And if Kate gave in now, she would disappear too. But it wouldn't be into a storm shelter. It would be into a deep grave somewhere in those woods.

"Can you run?" Kate whispered.

"I can do it," he said, his voice shaking slightly.

Without warning, she stepped back hard, using her body to shove Erik through the open shed doorway. Kate heard him stumble, then fall, as she turned and flew through the door, praying she would be able to shut it before Georgia got a shot off.

She wasn't.

27

The crack of the rifle firing sounded just before Kate slammed the door shut. The bullet plowed through the door, splinters shooting off and a hole erupting where it pierced it. A resultant narrow beam of light streamed inside, highlighting the dust puffed into the air from a mulch sack struck by the bullet.

"What are we doing?" Erik asked, his breathing labored. "She'll be here—"

"Stay down," Kate snapped, quickly rolling the wheelbarrow to block the door. Then she hustled to the back side of the shed where she pulled two loose boards off the wall, sending the frigid wind rushing in.

"Go on, through there," she urged.

Erik obeyed without argument, with Kate right behind him. Once outside, she grabbed his hand, dragging him through the increasingly blinding snowfall into the woods.

The Vow

The tree-line was just a dozen or so feet from the shed, and they disappeared into it just as Kate heard Georgia banging on the shed door. Moving as fast as they could with Erik in socks, no shoes, and still disoriented, she heard Georgia scream behind them.

"Kate! Erik!" The pounding on the door continued, too loud for a fist, most likely the butt of the rifle. "Open this door! I mean it! I'll shoot again. There's no—"

Suddenly, Georgia went silent and Kate knew. Georgia had remembered.

Kate had hoped to get a decent head start by going through the secret "door" they had played with as children. Georgia probably hadn't used it in years. At least she hoped she hadn't. But they had barely been running a full minute before Georgia figured it out.

She didn't stop to look for Georgia because they couldn't afford to lose any of the lead they had on her. But as they scrambled over underbrush and between trees, they could hear her bellowing somewhere behind them. And it was getting louder and louder, which meant she was closing the gap.

"You can't get away, Kate! You're not taking him! Not now! He's mine! He left you!" Georgia bellowed.

"Erik, come on, hon. I know it's hard. But we've got to move faster," she said, grabbing his sleeve and pulling him forward, her heart thumping. He was falling practically every other step. She was sucking in gulps of frigid air that hurt her lungs, her rapid exhales sending out clouds of breath.

We won't get far like this. Maybe not even to the cabin before she reaches us.

Her stomach plummeted. Even if they did somehow

manage to beat her there, the keys to the cabin were sitting in her purse. On Georgia's kitchen counter.

Georgia's voice was louder now, and Kate could even hear her footfalls as she thrashed through the woods, a bad sign.

"You'll never make it!" Georgia screamed. "I'll reach you first!"

And Kate knew she was right.

28

Another booming crack sounded. Kate instinctively dropped to the ground as Erik went down in the snow beside her.

"Are you hit?" she cried.

"No. Are you?" he asked, clasping her face in his hands.

Kate shook her head. "Come on," she urged, standing up and trying to pull him along. "We've—"

"Wait! Kate, stop!" Erik said, resisting her. Her face snapped to his, Kate ready to yell at him to get moving. But she understood when she followed his gaze to Rex holding a rifle on Georgia, who was holding a rifle aimed at them. They formed a bizarre line of connect-the-dots through the trees, with her and Erik at the top, Georgia a dozen yards behind them, and Rex a dozen yards behind her.

"Rex, get out of here!" Georgia screamed. Her eyes went to the rifle he held. "Where did you get that?"

"Georgia, this is wrong. You were wrong. You lied to me."

She kept her rifle pointed at Kate and Erik though she

spoke to her brother. "Rex," she said, no longer screaming, but instead speaking with a forced measured quality, "You're not going to shoot me."

"I don't want to, but I will if I have to. If I have to do it to save them," he said, flicking the barrel at Kate and Erik. "I can hit you where it'll stop you but not really hurt you. You know I can."

Rex had been a crack shot ever since Pop taught him how to shoot when he was just a teenager. Kate knew that he absolutely could shoot to wound without causing fatal damage. Georgia knew it too.

"I told you why we had to do this, Rex," Georgia pleaded. "It's for Erik. It's to keep him safe. He's mine now. He loves me."

Rex shook his head slowly. "No, Georgia. You're the one he needs to be kept safe from. Put the gun down. It's your last chance before I shoot."

The thing about Rex was that he didn't have it in him to lie. He never had, for as long as Kate had known him. He hadn't even lied about Erik, despite clearly knowing about him being in the shed, because Kate had never actually discussed with Rex what had happened *to* Erik. Only that Erik had left her, which was true, in a way. So if Rex said he was going to shoot, he was going to shoot.

"Rex, please," Georgia begged.

"Put it down, Georgia," he replied. "One...two—"

Before Rex reached the count of three, Georgia dropped the rifle in the snow and sank to her knees, bawling and screaming at the sky as sirens sounded in the distance.

29

Kate spent two hours being interviewed by Detective Gibson, the sheriff's detective assigned to the case, before they finally transported her to the county medical center to be with Erik while he got a full work-up. The doctors declared him to be in decent shape with a diagnosis of malnutrition, a recent forearm break that was still healing, and bloodwork showing high levels of a tranquilizer.

As for what had happened during the last year, Erik had given a brief rundown to the deputies who arrived on the scene in response to the 9-1-1 call Kate had managed to make while escaping through the woods. But there were still a lot of unanswered questions. Once Erik was settled and sleeping, Kate headed back to the sheriff's department where Detective Gibson filled her in on their progress.

"We've been able to gather a good bit of information from Georgia. She's essentially crumbled under the pressure and is answering all our questions. Didn't even request an attorney," Detective Gibson said as he leaned over his desk on his forearms. "Georgia did start seeing your husband professionally about two years ago. She believes they developed some kind of romantic connection, but his files make it clear that was a one-sided thing. We'll be interviewing Erik to clarify, of course, but that's how it looks."

Kate rocked forward in her chair. "So what happened last December? How did she manage to take and keep him?"

"The short of it is that she ambushed him outside his office late in the day. She had a gun and threatened to hurt you if he didn't comply. She told him she had someone watching you, ready to kill you. After that, they brought him out here and kept him locked up and or drugged up to keep him from escaping."

"Who did she have watching me?"

"She hired an ex-con she knew from here named Kip Larimer. He was watching you at Georgia's cabin today, and saw you head to the shed. He got in touch with her on her way home, which is how she got to you so fast. He was about to take off after you when you ran for the woods, but Rex got to him first. He tied him up and left him in a closet, which is where we found him. Actually, that was one of the few things Rex did tell us.

"Larimer's not as chatty as Georgia, so we're letting him stew. But Georgia's basically told us everything we need to know. She had Larimer start watching you again a couple of weeks ago, when you let the lawyers know you were going to the cabin for Christmas, then selling it. Since Georgia was the one posing as Erik in his communications with everyone—even his lawyer—she found out. With Erik stashed here, she obviously didn't want you right next door, which is why she arranged the," he made air quotes, "'divorce settlement' so you'd have to sell the cabin. She couldn't bring Erik into the open if you might show up there. Fast forward to you coming for Christmas, and she had a real problem. She needed to know where you were at all times."

"So there really was a stalker, but it was this Larimer guy, not Bleeker?" Kate asked.

"Right."

"Was that how Georgia knew when I wasn't home last Christmas? How she got in our house to plant that note in my tree?"

"Actually, she had Larimer plant it, after she forced Erik to write it."

Something wasn't making sense for Kate. "But I actually spoke with Erik during the last year. It was just a few times, but during those calls he pushed for the divorce, told me about Miranda—his fake fiancé—and insisted on getting his share of our assets as soon as possible, which was why I had to sell the cabin."

"Well, the few times you spoke to him were also under threat of harm to him and to you. Georgia says the threat of harming you was what worried Erik the most. Larimer followed you, gathering photos and video, enough for Georgia to prove you were in danger. Erik did what she wanted in order to keep you safe."

"And the social media profiles?" Kate asked.

"All part of keeping up the illusion, so no one would realize he was missing."

"Well, she did a great job. I completely bought it," she said. A pang of guilt struck her core. *I should have known better.*

"Anyone would have bought it. It was a solid ruse," the detective said, but it didn't make Kate feel better.

"What was her end game? She couldn't hold a gun on Erik forever."

He shook his head. "Her first priority was to get you out of the picture, which meant getting you to sell the cabin. After that, she believed she could make Erik fall for her and convince him to stay of his own volition."

"That's crazy."

"Well, it's pretty clear she needs professional help. I'm not saying it was a good plan, just that it *was* her plan."

"So when I decided not to sell, that messed up her plans."

He nodded. "She had to get you to sell. Several things were already working for her. That campsite in the attic, for one—that was Rex, by the way. Georgia didn't know about it until you found it. Rex told her he just wanted to be close to your grandparents, in a place he'd always felt safe. And then there was the receipt you found."

"What's the explanation for that?"

He shrugged. "Don't have one yet. But we'll get it. Anyway, all of it pointed to a potentially dangerous stalker, and Georgia didn't have to do a thing to make that happen. Now, she did have Rex grab his stuff from your attic, thinking that would scare you even more once you realized it was gone."

"So was that her, banging on the door that night? Distracting me from Rex?"

"Actually, that was Erik. He'd gotten loose somehow—Georgia said Rex told her he must have left the door unlocked—and stumbled through the woods to your cabin."

The odd slow, heavy knocking came back to Kate, and

suddenly it made sense. Because a drugged but desperate person might knock exactly that way.

"Georgia had to go after him once she realized he was gone," the detective said. "Says you almost caught them and ruined everything."

"Only I didn't, and it scared me even more." She took a deep breath, trying to digest Rex's involvement. "So...Rex did know what was going on." Concern stirred in her belly. She didn't want him punished for this. "You need to know that Rex has...well...some intellectual differences that—"

Detective Gibson held up a hand. "We know about Rex, and we're familiar with his situation. We've got a medical professional on the way to advise us on how best to proceed with him."

Kate blew out slowly. "Well, that's good."

"The D.A. has worked out a deal with his attorney already. Nobody wants to see him serve time for this. He'll have some kind of conditional release requiring psychiatric support. It's clear he was being manipulated by Georgia. She even talked him into ransacking their cabin, hoping to further convince you the area wasn't safe, hoping it would push you into selling."

"It almost did," Kate said, glancing at her hands in her lap before looking back up. "But the writing on the mirror was what finally convinced me. Do you know who was responsible for that?"

"That's something else Georgia doesn't know. So we aren't sure yet."

Kate bit her lip. "What was her plan if I didn't sell?"

"She didn't come right out and say it, but I gather Larimer would have made you disappear. Permanently."

A heavy sadness washed over Kate, as the depth of Georgia's betrayal hit home. She brushed away a threatening tear. "So what happens now?"

"Honestly? We could use your help with Rex, if you're up for it."

At just after ten p.m., Kate sat at a metal table directly across from Rex in an interview room at the sheriff's department. Next to him sat the attorney appointed to him by the state for the time being, a young woman in a rumpled suit, likely called in after already turning in for the night. She looked as tired as Kate felt.

Kate's fingers gripped a paper cup full of mediocre coffee. An identical paper cup of hot chocolate—Kate had made sure they knew Rex didn't like coffee—sat undisturbed before him. He was as low as Kate had ever seen him, his entire body collapsed on itself, shoulders threatening to touch the table and hands in his lap, the only things he would look at.

Detective Gibson had asked her to try to get more information from Rex, because he had barely spoken to them at all. She wanted to help. She wanted answers too. But she had no idea how to get them. She was an emotional mess inside, and she was certain Rex was no better.

There were so many feelings. The joy of getting her husband back. The relief from learning he hadn't left her after all. The anger over a year wasted processing a rejection that never actually happened, with its misspent angst and depression. Rage at the thought of Erik being kidnapped and held against his will for an entire year. A whole year stolen from him. From them. Brokenness over the loss of someone she thought was a friend who was clearly in the throes of serious mental illness. But it was the guilt that was the worst. It clawed at her, accusing her of being a terrible wife. A wife that would lose faith so easily, even if there *was* evidence to support losing it.

If Rex was battling anything close to that range of emotions, it was no wonder he hadn't wanted to talk. Kate closed her eyes, settling her soul. There would be time to deal with all of that. But right now she needed to focus on Rex. She offered a silent prayer for peace and wisdom, then looked at him.

"Rex?" she said quietly. "I know what happened. I know it wasn't your idea."

Rex shook his head. His attorney was watching him closely, and Kate hoped she wouldn't interrupt. Since a deal had already been authorized for Rex, the consequences for anything he might say were limited. Interrupting would only make this harder.

"The detective said Georgia convinced you to go along with her plan," Kate prompted, but he didn't respond. She decided to come at it another way. "You know, it was brave, what you did, rescuing us like that. That had to be so hard."

Rex spoke, but his gaze stayed down. "I couldn't let her hurt you. Even though she's my sister."

"You did the right thing."

"It doesn't feel good, though," he mumbled, still avoiding Kate's stare. "And the right thing should feel good."

"Sometimes the right thing is hard, Rex. And hard things don't always feel good. Sometimes they even hurt." Kate paused, one hand reaching out toward Rex, palm open, as she chose her words carefully. "I need you to understand that I don't blame you for what happened to Erik."

He offered no indication that he heard her. She pressed on. "The detective said that before all this, Georgia had been visiting Erik in Nashville."

"She was helping him," he offered in monotone, regurgitating the story Georgia had fed him.

"I know Georgia told you that Erik was in danger—in danger because of me—but that Erik didn't think so."

Rex sniffed. "She said that Erik was confused. That you were treating him badly and hurting him, but Erik was too loyal to save himself. So we had to save him."

"You *know* me, Rex," Kate said, hearing the hint of pleading in her own voice. "You've known me most of my life. Why did you believe those things about me?"

His gaze briefly flicked to her from beneath lashes moist with tears before returning to his lap. "Georgia said you had changed. That you were mean. She said she loved Erik and that Erik loved her, but he just didn't realize it because you were controlling him and wouldn't let him go. So she saved him from himself."

"And she brought him here. To your cabin?"

He nodded. "And I helped her keep him safe."

"That's what the drugs were for? To keep him here so he would be safe?"

Rex nodded again. "She said Erik didn't understand. That it was for his own good, like when we have to give the horses shots they don't want for their own good. She said eventually we wouldn't have to use them anymore, once Erik understood. I thought I was helping him."

"I know, Rex. And I believe you."

The Vow

"You do?"

Kate nodded. "Detective Gibson told me you wouldn't say much, except that you realized something was wrong once I arrived at Pop's cabin. That you started to doubt what Georgia was telling you. Is that true?"

He bit his lip. "You weren't mean at all. You were just...you. The same as you'd always been. And when Erik overheard us talking about you being here, he wasn't scared of you at all. He was excited. He started yelling that he had to see you."

"He wasn't drugged?"

"We weren't using the drugs as much anymore because he'd calmed down in the last few months. But when he overheard us, he wanted to see you so bad. He kept pounding on the walls and throwing things at the door. Georgia said we had to start giving him the shots again. And I was supposed to. But I didn't."

"No?"

"Not like before. Not as much. And when I'd bring him his food, he'd tell me how much he wanted to see you and that he wanted to go home. That all I had to do was let him go next door..." His voice trailed off, shades of concern coloring his face.

"Rex—you're not in trouble for this, okay? But I need the truth. When I first got to my cabin, lots of things were out of place. And Mama K's perfume bottle and Pop's glasses were gone. Do you know what happened?"

His mouth turned down. "A while ago—like, in the summer—Georgia said you would come back eventually, even if it was just to sell the cabin. She asked me to move stuff around and take some things you would notice. She said it would make you want to sell the cabin even more." He sniffed. "I kept the bottle and glasses safe, though. I can give them back now."

Sympathy for him swelled within her. "Thank you, Rex. I'd really like that." She waited, giving him a moment to process before continuing. "Can I ask you about the blanket and other stuff in my attic, and the Christmas tree...that was you, wasn't it?"

He nodded. "I just wanted to be close to Pop and Mama K. I wanted things back like they were. It was my quiet place. I could go there and think."

"And Christmas night, when someone was banging on my door—did you come to take it all?"

He nodded. "Georgia told me to. But I lost the receipt, and she got really mad."

"Wait, how did you get that receipt?"

"It was in Erik's pocket when Georgia brought him here. She took his wedding ring, but she didn't know about the receipt. He kept it. Said it was his link to you. But I took it one time when she was really mad and searching the shelter because he tried to hurt her with a piece of wood he found. I thought she would take it away if she found it. But then I lost it in your attic anyway."

"Georgia said Erik was the one banging on my door. That he got out." She paused. "Do you know how that happened?"

"I thought, if maybe Erik could see you, we could work it all out. That maybe Georgia would see she was wrong. That he still loved you. So I left the shelter unlocked and gave him a really low dose of his shot that day. I told him I was sneaking in to get my things and he could follow me if he wanted to. Only he was so slow. The drugs must have still been too much. I came in the back of your cabin through the bedroom porch. I still have the key Pop gave me. You were asleep. I just went upstairs and was collecting everything, and that's when I heard the banging. I was afraid you'd see me leave, but you were really focused on the front door, yelling at it. You didn't even notice me come down the stairs behind you and go out the back."

"What happened to Erik?"

"Georgia saw the shed open and realized he'd gotten out. Then her friend called her to tell her Erik was on your porch. She has a friend that's been following you to make sure you're safe."

"I know, Rex." Of course Georgia would tell him Larimer was following Kate for her own good.

"But I didn't disobey her. I was a good brother. Erik left all by himself."

So he had rationalized going against Georgia's wishes by letting Erik be the one to choose to leave.

Poor guy. Manipulation isn't a strong enough word for how Georgia took advantage of him.

Kate thought back on how Rex had always been so tense whenever Erik's name came up. She had assumed he was angry at Erik for leaving her, but it was clear now that Rex's reaction was due to everything going on behind the scenes. All she wanted to do was gather him into a hug. "It wasn't your fault, Rex. None of it was."

"Well, Georgia said *that* part was my fault. And that she had to grab Erik off your porch, and you almost caught them, and that would have ruined everything. After that, she didn't let me see Erik alone anymore."

"Rex...the message on my mirror—that was you, wasn't it?" Kate pressed.

He nodded again. "I remembered that one time Erik said he just needed to get a message to you. He needed you to know that he wasn't gone. That he didn't leave you. So I thought I should do that for him."

"Why did you write it in lipstick on my mirror?"

Rex shrugged. "I had to make sure you saw it. I saw somebody do that in a movie once."

Kate couldn't keep the corner of her mouth from rising a little. "And you took my rifle too? Pop's rifle?"

"I was afraid you might shoot Georgia with it if she tried to bring you to the cabin like she brought Erik. Or that you might accidentally shoot Erik if he got out again. Or me, if I needed to come into your cabin again. Plus, Georgia wouldn't let me have my own gun. She kept them locked up. I thought I might need one."

This time Kate had to smile. "Well, it's a good thing you took it," she said, thinking of Rex holding that rifle on Georgia in the woods.

"I guess so," Rex answered. Though he didn't smile, he did finally look her in the eye.

"Why didn't you just tell me what was going on? Were you afraid of Georgia?"

He shook his head. "She's my older sister. She takes care of me. I have to obey her. She told me not to tell, so I didn't."

"But the other things—leaving the shed open, not giving Erik full doses of his shots, and leaving that message on the mirror—you could do those things because it wasn't disobeying? Because she hadn't specifically told you not to do them?"

Relief flooded his eyes. "Yes," he said, looking at her like a drowning person who had just been thrown a life preserver.

"When I went into your cabin to clean up, Rex, there were

some things I thought were kind of strange. Georgia's psychiatric file, the file from Erik's office, was laying out for anyone to see. She didn't leave it there, did she? That was you. You put it there when I told you I was coming to clean up."

He nodded ever so slightly.

"You were hoping I'd find it?"

He nodded again.

"I also thought it was odd that her laptop was unlocked—did you do something to it?"

"I know her password. I put it in and changed the setting so it wouldn't lock again." He angled a little toward his attorney for the first time. "I'm not very good with people, but I'm real good with machines and animals and computers and stuff like that."

His attorney smiled. "I'm sure you are, Rex."

"People are confusing sometimes, aren't they?" Kate asked.

"People don't always tell the truth," he said. "They don't always say what they mean."

"No, they don't." She inhaled slowly. "Rex, I want to ask you one more thing and then I'll be done, okay?"

"Okay."

"The keys you gave me when I came to clean—you gave me all of them on purpose, didn't you? So I could get in the shed if I figured it out. So I could save Erik?"

"Yes." He sniffed. "And I know Georgia wouldn't have wanted me to do any of those things, but she, she..." He faltered momentarily. "She wasn't right. Like she was the confused one for once, not me."

"She *was* confused, Rex. You were right. And I'm so glad you did what you did."

"Can I see her?"

Kate exchanged a knowing look with the attorney. She doubted Rex would see his sister anytime soon.

"I don't know, Rex. You have to understand that what Georgia did was really wrong."

"She's in a lot of trouble, isn't she?"

"Yes, she is. But they're going to get her the help she needs so she isn't confused anymore."

"I guess that's a good thing," he said.

"It is."

Slowly, tentatively, he reached a hand out to grasp Kate's still outstretched one. "And sometimes the good things are hard."

30

"It's perfect," Kate said, watching Erik on the ladder, placing her grandparents' star on top of their tree in their cabin, exactly how it should be.

He stepped down, pulled her close and kissed her, his auburn beard tickling her. "It is."

The fire crackled behind them as Kate's gaze drifted to Rex, sitting on the floor playing with the Golden Retriever puppy Erik had given her for Christmas. Rex was laughing, something she hadn't seen him do very often.

"Thank you for letting him be a part of this," Kate whispered. "It means a lot to him."

"It means a lot to me," Erik replied, running his fingers through the blond hair cascading down her back. "He's the reason I'm here with you. I just hope he can handle all the people once your family gets here."

"He'll be fine. He knows and loves them. Besides, his counselor said social interaction is important," Kate added.

A few months after her arrest, Georgia was convicted of

kidnapping and several other offenses, and was now serving a long prison sentence. Rex's deal put him on probation, conditional on him remaining in counseling for several years. The counselor worked with Rex to make sure he understood what had happened, why it was wrong, and to ensure nothing like it happened again. Erik and Kate stayed in regular contact with both the counselor and Rex. At this point, they were the closest thing to family he had. They had made trips to the cabin throughout the year to visit him, and once he had even come back to Nashville with them for a few days. And when he needed to visit Georgia, they were the ones who took him.

Kate's gaze drifted to the fire as Erik wrapped his arms around her waist. "I can't believe it's been a year. Sometimes I still can't believe you're back." Even as she said it, a familiar darkness seeped into her spirit, as it often did when her thoughts turned to those memories.

"Why do you do that?" Erik asked.

"Do what?"

"It's like you shrivel a little whenever we talk about it."

So I haven't been as good at hiding my feelings as I thought. She had hoped she would work through it on her own. She preferred not to discuss it with him because she hated to admit it to herself, much less to him. But maybe there was no avoiding it.

She sighed. "It's just that I feel so...guilty for believing you would leave. I didn't go looking for you. I didn't send anyone to check on you. I just...believed it."

Erik turned to face her. "Kate, Georgia's lie was well-constructed. I don't blame you for believing it. I would have believed it too. You have to stop blaming yourself."

Moisture gathered in Kate's eyes.

"I see it in you. Like something holding you down, keeping you from being free." He clasped her face with his hands. "It's Christmas, Kate. And my gift to you is me saying, let it go. Until you do, you're just holding yourself hostage."

She pressed her head against his chest. "I should have known better. I hate that I doubted you. No matter how good a job Georgia did."

"You didn't do anything wrong, and I don't need you to beat yourself up or pay some kind of penance. Do you think God wants you living this way, when he's given us a second chance?"

He was right. Clinging to the guilt, beating herself up, was her way of paying penance for the betrayal she believed she committed. If she did it long enough, felt bad enough, maybe someday she could let it go. But that wasn't living. And it certainly wasn't the abundant life God wanted for her. The only one requiring it of her...was her.

"You're right," she said, and found she meant it. "I'll let it go."

"You mean it?"

She felt a smile crease her face. "I mean it."

He grinned back. "Promise?"

She rubbed her thumb over his wedding ring and leaned into his embrace.

"I do."

ACKNOWLEDGMENTS

Thank you to —

My readers, for choosing to read my stories and share them with others. It means more than you know.

My dedicated beta readers: Linda Sproul, Debbie Lott, Laura Stratton, Gene Gettler, Shaw Gookin, Tessa Hobbs, Kirsten Harbers, and Tijuana Collier. You guys help me get it right.

My editor, Kim Kemery. I'm so grateful for your attention to detail.

My friend, fellow author, and mentor, Luana Ehrlich. I owe you so much.

My parents, Lynn and Bob Plummer, who taught me to read and birthed my love of stories.

NOTE TO MY READERS

I hope you enjoyed *The Vow*, the first of three stand-alone books in The Deadly Decisions Collection. If you did, please tell your friends and leave a rating and review wherever you shop for books, on Amazon, Goodreads, and Bookbub, and/or mention it on whatever social media platforms you enjoy. Pick any or all. Reviews and word of mouth are what keep a novelist's work alive, and I would be extremely grateful for yours.

Would you like a free, award-winning short story?

Visit my website at www.dlwoodonline.com to learn about my books and subscribe to my newsletter, which will keep you updated (usually only twice a month) on free and discounted goodies, new releases, advance review team opportunities and more.

ABOUT D.L. WOOD

D.L. Wood is a *USA TODAY* and Amazon bestselling author who writes thrilling suspense laced with romance and faith. Her novels strive to give readers the same thing she wants: a "can't-put-it-down-stay-up-till-3am" character-driven story full of heart, believability, and adrenaline. Her award-winning books offer clean captivating fiction that entertains *and* uplifts.

D.L. lives in North Alabama, where, if she isn't writing, you'll probably catch her curled up with a cup of Earl Grey, bingeing on the latest BBC detective series. If you have one to recommend, please email her immediately, because she's nearly exhausted the ones she knows about. She loves to hear from readers, and you can reach her at:

dlwood@dlwoodonline.com

FOLLOW AUTHOR D.L. WOOD

It's a tremendous help to authors when readers follow us on social media. Don't miss a thing —follow me on these platforms so you'll know about my latest releases, bargains and more. Thank you!

Facebook
https://facebook.com/dlwoodonline
Goodreads
https://www.goodreads.com/dlwood
Bookbub
https://www.bookbub.com/authors/d-l-wood
Twitter
https://www.twitter.com/dlwoodonline
Amazon
https://amazon.com/D.L.-Wood/e/B0165NBAMC
YouTube
https://youtube.com/channel/UCMYV7dogFR49f_ZobZnahOA

SECRETS AND LIES ARE DANGEROUS THINGS

Boston police detective Dani Lake dreads returning to her hometown of Skye, Alabama, for her 10-year high school reunion. But not for the normal reasons.

At fifteen, Dani discovered the body of her classmate, and her failure to provide evidence leading to the killer resulted in the unjust conviction of her dear friend and a guilt burden she carried for life. When new evidence is unearthed during her visit, suggesting the truth she's always suspected, she embarks on a mission to expose the killer, aided by police detective Chris Newton, who just happens to be the man Dani's best friend is dying to set her up with, and the only person who believes her.

But when Dani pushes too hard, someone pushes back, endangering Dani and those closest to her as she uncovers secrets deeper and darker than she ever expected to learn—secrets that may bring the truth to light, if they don't get her killed first.

SECRETS SHE KNEW is the first of the stand-alone *Secrets and Lies Suspense Novels*.

GET YOUR COPY AND START READING NOW

BONUS EXCERPT FROM
UNINTENDED TARGET

Have you tried D.L. Wood's *Unintended Series?* On the following pages is an excerpt from **UNINTENDED TARGET**, the first novel in this series which has captivated readers, with nearly 4 million pages read on Kindle Unlimited alone and an Illumination Awards Gold Medal for Best Christian Fiction ebook.

This series follows Chloe McConnaughey, an unsuspecting travel photojournalist, thrust into harrowing and mysterious circumstances ripe with murder, mayhem, and more. And by more, I mean a handsome man or two that seem too good to be true—and just might be. Turn to the next page to get started.

Amazon Reviews for UNINTENDED TARGET

"D.L. Wood truly does know how to captivate her readers; a master storyteller."

"Just the right balance of intrigue and a touch of romance."

"All I can say is buckle up, it's gonna be intense."

"Best book I have read in a while."

"It has been a long time since I stayed up until 3 am to finish a book in one sitting!"

"This book had all the components of an engrossing read...mystery, romance and best of all, great writing."

Goodreads Reviews for UNINTENDED TARGET

"...[A] story on steroids as it never let up with more twists and turns than I can remember."

"You can't find a book with more fast paced suspense than this one."

"I highly recommend not reading this book before bed, you'll not want to put it down."

"...twists and turns to entertain even the most demanding reader."

CHAPTER ONE

"He's done it again," groaned Chloe McConnaughey, her cell held to her ear by her shoulder as she pulled one final pair of shorts out of her dresser. "Tate knew that I had to leave by 3:30 at the latest. I sent him a text. I know he got it," she said, crossing her bedroom to the duffel bag sitting on her four-poster bed and tossing in the shorts.

Her best friend's voice rang sympathetically out of the phone. "There's another flight out tomorrow," offered Izzie Morales hesitantly.

Chloe zipped up the bag. "I know," she said sadly. "But, that isn't the point. As usual, it's all about Tate. It doesn't matter to him that I'm supposed to be landing on St. Gideon in six hours. What does an assignment in the Caribbean matter when your estranged brother decides it's time to finally get together?"

"Estranged is a bit of a stretch, don't you think?" Izzie asked.

"It's been three months. No texts. No calls. Nothing," Chloe replied, turning to sit on the bed.

"You know Tate. He gets like this. He doesn't mean anything by it. He just got... distracted," Izzie offered.

"For three months?"

Izzie changed gears. "Well, it's only 3:00—maybe he'll show."

"And we'll have, what, like thirty minutes before I have to go?" Chloe grunted in frustration. "What's the point?"

"Come on," Izzie said, "The point is, maybe this gets repaired."

Chloe sighed. "I know. I know," she said resignedly. "That's why I'm waiting it out." She paused. "He said he had news he didn't want to share over the phone. Seriously, what kind of news can't you share over the phone?"

"Maybe it's so good that he just has to tell you in person," Izzie suggested hopefully.

"Or maybe it's—'I've been fired again, and I need a place to crash.'"

"Think positively," Izzie encouraged, and Chloe heard a faint tap-tapping in the receiver. She pictured her friend on the other side of Atlanta, drumming a perfectly manicured, red-tipped finger on a nearby surface, her long, pitch-colored hair hanging in straight, silky swaths on either side of her face.

"He'll probably pull up any minute, dying to see you," Izzie urged. "And if he's late, you can reschedule your flight for tomorrow. Perk of having your boss as your best friend. I'll authorize the magazine to pay for the ticket change. Unavoidable family emergency, right?"

Chloe sighed again, picked up the duffel bag and started down the hall of her two-bedroom rental. "I just wish it wasn't this hard." The distance between them hadn't been her choice and she hated it. "Ten to one he calls to say he's had a change of plans, too busy with work, can't make it."

"He won't," replied Izzie.

With a thud, Chloe dropped the bag onto the kitchen floor by the door to the garage, trading it for half a glass of merlot perched on the counter. She took a small sip. "Don't underestimate him. His over-achievement extends to every part of his life, including his ability to disappoint."

"Ouch." Izzie paused. "You know, Chlo, it's just the job."

"I have a job. And somehow I manage to answer my calls."

"But your schedule's a little more your own, right? Pressure-wise I think he's got a little bit more to worry about."

Chloe rolled her eyes. "Nice try. But he manages tech security at an investment firm, not the White House. It's the same thing every time. He's totally consumed."

"Well, speaking as your editor, being a *little* consumed by your job is not always a bad thing."

"Ha-ha."

"What's important is that he's trying to reconnect now."

Chloe brushed at a dust bunny clinging to her white tee shirt, flicking it to the floor. "What if he really has lost this job? It took him two years after the lawsuit to find this one."

"Look, maybe it's a promotion. Maybe he got a bonus, and he's finally setting you up. Hey, maybe he's already bought you that mansion in Ansley Park..."

"I don't *need* him to set me up—I'm not eight years old anymore. I'm fine now. I wish he'd just drop the 'big-brother-takes-care-of-wounded-little-sister' thing. He's the wounded one."

"You know, if you don't lighten up a bit, it may be another three months before he comes back to see you."

"One more day and he wouldn't have caught me at all."

Izzie groaned jealously. "It's not fair that you get to go and I have to stay. It's supposed to be thirty-nine and rainy in Atlanta for, like, the next month."

"So come along."

"If only. You know I can't. Zach's got his school play next weekend. And Dan would kill me if I left him with Anna for more than a couple days right now." A squeal sounded on Izzie's end. "Uggggh. I think Anna just bit Zach again. I've gotta go. Don't forget to call me tomorrow and let me know how it went with big brother."

"Bigger by just three minutes," she quickly pointed out. "And I'll try to text you between massages in the beach-side cabana."

Izzie groaned again, drowning out another squeal in the background. "You're sick."

"It's a gift," Chloe retorted impishly before hanging up.

Chloe stared down at the duffel and, next to it, the special backpack holding her photography equipment. She double-checked the *Terra Traveler* I.D. tags on both and found all her information still legible and secure. "Now what?" she muttered.

Her stomach rumbled, reminding her that, with all the packing and preparation for leaving the house for two weeks, she had forgotten to eat. Rummaging through the fridge, she found a two-day old container of Chinese take-out. Tate absolutely hated Chinese food. She loved it. Her mouth curved at the edges as she shut the refrigerator door. *And that's the least of our differences.*

Leaning against the counter, she cracked open the container and used her chopsticks to pluck julienne carrots out of her sweet and sour chicken. *Too bad Jonah's not here,* she thought, dropping the orange slivers distastefully into the sink. *Crazy dog eats anything. Would've scarfed them down in half a second.* But the golden retriever that was her only roommate was bunking at the kennel now. She missed him already. She felt bad about leaving him for two whole weeks. Usually her trips as a travel journalist for *Terra Traveler* were much shorter, but she'd tacked on some vacation time to this one in order to do some work on her personal book project. She wished she had someone she could leave him with, but Izzie was her only close friend, and she had her hands full with her kids.

Jonah would definitely be easier than those two, she thought with a smile. He definitely had been the easiest and most dependable roommate she'd ever had—and the only male that had never let her down. A loyal friend through a bad patch of three lousy boyfriends. The last of them consumed twelve months of her life before taking her "ring-shopping," only to announce the next day that he was leaving her for his ex. It had taken six months, dozens of amateur therapy sessions with Izzie and exceeding the limit on her VISA more than once to get over that one. After that she'd sworn off men for the foreseeable future, except for Jonah of course, which, actually, he seemed quite pleased about.

She shoveled in the last few bites of fried rice, then tossed the box into the trash. *Come to think of it,* she considered as she headed for the living room, *Tate'll be the first man to step inside this house in almost a year.* She wasn't sure whether that was empowering or pathetic.

"Not going there," she told herself, forcing her train of thought instead to the sunny beaches of St. Gideon. The all-expenses paid jaunts were the only real perks of her job as a staff journalist with *Terra Traveler,* an online travel magazine based out of Atlanta. They were also the only reason she'd stayed on for the last four years despite her abysmal pay. Photography, her real passion, had never even paid the grocery bill, much less the rent. Often times the trips offered some truly unique spots to shoot in. Odd little places like the "World's Largest Tree House," tucked away in the Smoky Mountains, or the home of the largest outdoor collection of ice sculptures in a tiny town in Iceland. And sometimes she caught a real gem, like this trip to the Caribbean. Sun, sand, and separation from everything stressful. For two whole weeks.

The thought of being stress-free reminded her that at this particular moment, she wasn't. Frustration flared as she thought of Tate's text just an hour before:

Flying in tonite. Ur place @ 2. Big news. See u then.

Typical Tate. No advance warning. No, *"I'm sorry I haven't returned a single call in three months"* or *"Surprise, I haven't fallen off the face of the earth. Wanna get together?"* Just a demand.

A familiar knot of resentment tightened in her chest as she took her wine into the living room, turned up Adele on the stereo and plopped onto a slipcovered couch facing the fire. Several dog-eared books were stacked near the armrest, and she pushed them aside to make room as she sank into the loosely stuffed cushions. She drew her favorite quilt around her, a mismatched pink and beige patchwork that melded perfectly with the hodgepodge of antique and shabby chic furnishings that filled the room.

What do you say to a brother who by all appearances has intentionally ignored you for months? It's one thing for two friends to become engrossed in their own lives and lose track of each other for a while. It's something else altogether when your twin brother doesn't return your calls. He hadn't been ill, although that had been her first thought. After the first few weeks she got a text from him saying, *sorry, so busy, talk to u ltr*. So she had called his office just to make sure he was still going in. He was. He didn't take her call that day either.

She tried to remember how many times she'd heard "big news" from Tate before, but quickly realized she'd lost count years ago. A pang of pity slipped in beside the frustration, wearing away at its edges.

She set her goblet down on the end table beside a framed picture of Tate. In many respects it might as well have been a mirror. They shared the same large amber eyes and tawny hair, though she let her loose curls grow to just below her narrow shoulders. Their oval faces and fair skin could've been photocopied they were so similar. But he was taller and stockier, significantly out-sizing her petite, five foot four frame. She ran a finger along the faint, half-inch scar just below her chin that also differentiated them. He'd given her that in a particularly fierce game of keep-away when they were six. Later, disappointed that she had an identifying mark he didn't, he had unsuccessfully tried duplicating the scar by giving himself a nasty paper cut. In her teenage years she'd detested the thin, raised line, but now she rubbed it fondly, feeling that in some small, strange way it linked her to him.

He had broken her heart more than a little, the way he'd shut her out since taking the position at Inverse Financial nearly a year ago. He'd always been the type to throw himself completely into what he was doing, but this time he'd taken his devotion to a new high, allowing it to alienate everyone and everything in his life.

It hadn't always been that way. At least not with her. They'd grown up close, always each other's best friend and champion. Each other's only champion, really. It was how they survived the day after their eighth birthday when their father, a small-time attorney, ran off to North Carolina with the office copy lady. That was when Tate had snuck into their mother's bedroom, found a half-used box of Kleenex and brought it to Chloe as she hid behind the winter clothes in her closet. *I'll always take care of you, Chlo. Don't cry. I'm big enough to take care of both of us.* He'd said it with so much conviction that she'd believed him.

Together they'd gotten through the day nine months after that when the divorce settlement forced them out of their two-story Colonial into an orange rancher in the projects. Together they weathered their mother's alcoholism that didn't make her mean, just tragic, and finally, just dead, forcing them into foster homes. And though they didn't find any love there, they did manage to stay together for the year and a half till they turned eighteen.

Then he went to Georgia Tech on a scholarship and she, still at a loss for what she wanted to do in life, took odd jobs in the city. The teeny one bedroom apartment they shared seemed like their very own castle. After a couple of years, he convinced her she was going nowhere without a degree, so she started at the University of Georgia. For the first time they were separated. But Athens was only a couple hours away and he visited when he could and still paid for everything financial aid didn't. She'd tried to convince him she could make it on her own, but he never listened, still determined to be the provider their father had never been.

When she graduated, she moved back to Atlanta with her journalism degree under her belt and started out as a copy editor for a local events magazine. Tate got his masters in computer engineering at the same time and snagged a highly competitive job as a software designer for an up-and-coming software development company. It didn't take long for them to recognize Tate's brilliance at anything with code, and the promotions seemed to come one after the other.

Things had been so good then. They were both happy, both making money, though she was only making a little and he, more and more as time went by. The photo in her hands had been taken back then, when the world was his for the taking. Before it all fell apart for him with that one twist of fate that had ruined everything—

Stop, she told herself, shaking off the unpleasant memory. The whole episode had nearly killed Tate, and she didn't like to dwell on it. It had left him practically suicidal until, finally, this Inverse job came along. When it did, she thought that everything would get better, that things would just go back to normal. But they didn't. Instead Tate had just slowly disappeared from her life, consumed by making his career work...

She brushed his frozen smile with her fingers. Affection and pity and a need for the only person who had ever made her feel like she was a part of something special swelled, finally beating out the aggravation she had been indulging. As she set the frame back on the table, her phone rang. *Speak of the devil*, she thought, smiling as she reached for her cell.

"Hello?"

A deep, tentative voice that did not belong to her brother answered.

* * * * *

It never ceased to amaze him how death could be so close to a person without them sensing it at all. Four hours had passed and she hadn't noticed a thing. It was dark now, and rain that was turning to sleet ticked steadily on the car, draping him in a curtain of sound as he watched her vague grey shadow float back and forth against the glow of her drawn Roman blinds. He was invisible here, hunkered down across the street behind the tinted windows of his dark Chevy Impala, swathed in the added darkness of the thick oaks lining the neighbor's yard.

Invisible eyes watching. Waiting.

Watch. Wait. Simple enough instructions. But more were coming. Out of habit he felt the Glock cradled in his jacket and fleetingly wondered *why* he was watching her, before quickly realizing he didn't care. He wasn't paid to wonder.

He was just a hired gun. A temporary fix until the big guns arrived. But, even so...

He scanned the yard. The dog was gone. She was completely alone. *It would be, oh, so easy.*

But he was being paid to watch. Nothing more.

Her shadow danced incessantly from one end of the room to the other. Apparently the news had her pacing.

What would she do if she knew she was one phone call away from never making a shadow dance again?

THE STORY CONTINUES IN
UNINTENDED TARGET

GET YOUR COPY AND START READING NOW

BOOKS BY D.L. WOOD

THE UNINTENDED SERIES
Unintended Target
Unintended Witness
Unintended Detour

THE CRIMINAL COLLECTION
A Criminal Game
A Criminal Web (Coming Soon)

THE SECRETS AND LIES SUSPENSE NOVELS
Secrets She Knew
Liar Like Her

THE DEADLY DECISIONS COLLECTION
The Vow
The Offer (Coming Soon)
The Choice (Coming Soon)

Printed in Great Britain
by Amazon